HAND-TO-HAND!

I would have exchanged the empty Colt for a fresh one but things were happening too fast and Ellie was still loading the one I had given her. What appeared to be the last of the dismounted Comanches was making his way to Old Bob now. He had a hunting knife in his hand, ready to kill the Ranger and scalp him right then and there. I only had one weapon in reach and I used it. The brave was about to ram his knife into Bob's side when my Colt found him. . . .

COMANCHE TRAIL

THE COLT REVOLVER NOVELS

Jim Miller

SEVERN
SH
HOUSE

This title first published in Great Britain 1988 by
SEVERN HOUSE PUBLISHERS LTD of
40–42 William IV Street, London WC2N 4DF
by arrangement with Ballantine Books,
a division of Random House, Inc., New York

British Library Cataloguing in Publication Data
Miller, Jim
Comanche trail.
Rn: James L. Collins   I. Title
813'.54[F]
ISBN 0–7278–1671–3

Printed and bound in Great Britain

To Jim Norland,
for saving my bacon
a time or two.

Chapter One

There ain't no such thing as living happily ever after. It's pure storybook stuff and I told Finn as much. All he did was smile at me like I didn't know what I was talking about. But time proved me right, even if he never did admit to it.

After the Battle of San Jacinto, I took Ellie back to Hartford and married her, showing her off to Ma and Pa all the while. They took a shine to each other right quick, Ellie and my folks, and I knew that kind of made Ma feel better when we left that time, knowing that when Finn and me got back to Texas we would have a woman to look after us. And maybe she was right in a way. I never did take a liking to washing clothes and such, which was why I had chosen buckskins to wear when I first ventured onto the Texas frontier. Just wear them until they fall off or until you can find an ant hill to spread them out over to get rid of the lice and such. It was as simple as that. But Ma must have figured that Ellie would make an honest man out of me, and that she did.

Finn and me picked out a site not too far from Bexar of what people were starting to call San Antonio now that the population was on the increase. And that's when I said what I did to Finn, for it is no easy chore to build a ranch, much less a ranch house, with only two men. There was always something that had to be taken care of, and I won't deny that I was far from happy when I was doing those chores. Add to it the fact that Ellie gave birth to James, our first son, in '37, and Finn and me were members of the Rangers and spent a good amount of our time chasing Comanches and others who had no particular use for the new American settlers, and you can see how much work was not getting done.

In a way, all that Indian activity was responsible for me now being in New York and sitting across the table from Sam Colt in the summer of '40. I could only spend a couple of days with him before returning to Texas, and I tried to pump as much information from him as I could in that short time span.

"Your Sam Walker is a convincing man, Nate," Colt said, finishing his meal. Sam Walker had come to Texas just after the Revolution and joined the Rangers. He had fought in the Black Hawk and Seminole wars down in the Florida Territory earlier and had established a reputation as an Indian fighter in his own right. As a Ranger he had a chance to use Sam Colt's Paterson Model and had taken a special interest in the weapon as a possible cavalry arm. And when you came right down to it, there weren't any cavalry on the face of the earth that were better at fighting on horseback than the Comanches. Except, maybe, the Rangers. Sam knew it as well as anyone and he did something about it.

"When he was here last fall, I was surprised how much he knew about weapons, especially my own,"

Sam continued. "And his suggestions made a lot of sense, particularly after he told me about the Indian trouble you have out there. In fact, I got a patent on that lever rammer he suggested shortly after he left. Now, if I can get the army to take a look at this new model, I might be able to get a contract with them."

"More coffee, gentlemen?" the waitress asked before I could say anything. She was a pretty young lady with black hair and eyes to match, and polite and well mannered as anyone I had seen of late. But then, this was one of the better restaurants in the city according to Sam, so maybe I should have expected all that anyway. I had not paid much attention to her until now, when I noticed that she was acting like she hardly knew Sam was there, instead smiling her hardest at me. Now, I'm not too awful good around women, and I don't mind saying that this one made me feel kind of uneasy just being there. When she winked at me and smiled again before turning to go, I knew she would be trouble if I were to stay. It made me glad I was leaving next morning.

"She seems to have taken a fancy to you," Sam said, watching her walk away.

"Then I hope it's just a passing fancy," I said, taking a gulp of my coffee. "Getting these pistols back to Texas all in one piece is gonna be hard enough without woman trouble." I had seen women like that before, the kind who flirt and tease a man but have no honest intentions toward him. Out west most of them were found in bars and cantinas and the red light district, so in a way it surprised me to find such a woman in a place Sam spoke of as one of the city's better restaurants. Or maybe it was just the way of things in the east. But east or west, I knew when trouble was afoot and I was about to mention to Sam that it was time to call it a night, for more and more I was getting the urge to leave this place, no matter how good the food was.

But I did not get the chance.

The door to the establishment flew open and would have busted the fancy wording and design of its glass had it swung any harder. Instead it bounced back off its hinges as the man who had pushed it walked in just as abruptly. He was dressed in the garrison uniform of a soldier, minus the headgear, a sergeant by the look of the chevrons on his arm. He was as big as me and just as ugly, even more so. He had the height of an Englishman and the thickness of an Irishman who's spent a good share of his life fighting, and perhaps a bit of the Moor somewhere in his bloodline, for his skin had a tint to it that was a shade darker than most. Or it could have been the whiskey he'd been drinking that gave him the flush. It sure didn't make him look any friendlier, and the disoriented glaze in his eyes told me that drunk or not this man was on the prod, just looking for trouble.

I pushed my chair back. "Sam, let's get out of here," I said, trying to sound as casual as I could. "I've got to leave before daybreak tomorrow and I might as well get a decent night's rest before I do."

Right then I knew there was going to be trouble.

Sometimes you get a gut feeling and it only takes a split second to know it's right, and that's what happened to me while I was getting up. I don't know how, but something told me that the pretty waitress and the big man in the doorway knew each other. I knew it for sure when she looked at me again and made sure everyone saw that wink of hers. The drunk saw her, took several steps until he was at her side, grabbed her arm, saying, "There you are," and took to cussing her. It didn't take much to see that the grip on her arm was painful and when she asked him to let go and he refused, she slapped him so hard in the face that for a second it seemed to be all you could hear in there. It infuriated him and he brought his huge hand back.

At the same time I was moving across the floor, catching his wrist in my own hand as he was about to strike her. I kicked a foot out from behind him as my own body struck him from the side. It threw him off-balance and he fell to the floor, careening off a chair as he did.

"You do something like that down in Texas, mister, and they'd horsewhip you," I said as he got his senses back and looked at me in that unbelieving way a drunk will. But it didn't take him long to remember what had happened. I don't know what he had at his side, but as soon as his hand started moving across his belt, I was pulling out my own bowie knife.

"Sirs!"

It was said loud enough to get our attention, and if that wasn't enough, the cocking of the horse pistol sure did it. A quick glance and I saw what must have been the owner of this eatery standing next to the waitress, pistol in hand, a grim, determined look on his face.

"There will be no fighting or bloodshed under my roof, gentlemen. I want that understood." He had a foreign accent, but I wasn't about to argue with the business end of a horse pistol, so I just nodded to him while Sam paid the bill and the drunk got to his feet. All the while, the girl seemed to be enjoying the whole show, like it was being put on for her benefit alone.

The soldier still looked like he was out for blood and wasn't about to stop until he had some. I knew well enough that when a man made a fool of himself, he was likely to get vengeful in the way he looked at things. And if he was drunk to boot, well, he would probably get careless as well. It was what Finn called flustered, which he described as having seventeen different ways to react to something and not knowing which one to pick. And this sergeant was flustered. Besides, he didn't show too much as a fighter. So I gave him a knowing smile before I walked out that door, knowing he would follow.

As soon as I was out the door, I stepped to one side of it. The sun was down and the street lighting was poor, but I knew from the way he had entered that he would leave in the same tirade that could be heard before it was seen at least a block away. I hit him full in the middle when he came staggering out, right where the ribs separate, and it knocked the wind out of him. When he doubled over, I grabbed him by the seat of the pants and nape of his neck and pushed him forward hard enough to roll down the steps and into the street. He landed flat on his back and would have reached across his waist again, but I put a heavy boot down on his hand before he could move.

"You take to grudge fighting in your shape, friend, and you're never gonna live long enough to appreciate living," I said.

"How dashing." The waitress was now standing on the boardwalk while a crowd of sorts began to gather, and I got the idea she was enjoying the attention. "And all for a lady's honor," she added, smiling.

I was getting as mad at her as I had been with the drunk and decided it was time she knew it.

"Not hardly," I said, loud enough for all to hear. "Besides, you cause the kind of ruckus you just did down where I come from, and there ain't nobody in a hundred miles would call you a *lady*."

She didn't have the smugness about her now that she did before and I thought sure her jaw would drop clean down to her belly button with the expression she now had on her face. And if Sam hadn't yanked me away from her right then, I do believe I would have felt the sting of her hand as much as the drunk did.

"You'll excuse us, please," Sam said to anyone who was listening. "We have to be going now." He sounded kind of nervous the way he said it, as though he figured the rest of the army would be there momentarily to avenge what happened to the soldier.

We were about a block away when he glanced at me as though I had started the whole affair.

"Nathan, why is it that whenever you leave here, you're always in trouble?" he asked.

I had to smile at Sam's impatience, for other than the time I had spent with him, the night's events had been the most fun I had had since coming east.

"Reckon I'm just born to it, Sam. Just born to it."

Chapter Two

I said my good-byes to Caroline and Sam that night and by daybreak the next morning was on my way. On my lonesome it would take maybe a week to get to Texas, but with the Conestoga full of weapons I had, well, a month might be closer to it. There was no reason to be in a hurry, yet I knew the Rangers were a bit more than anxious to get their hands on Sam Colt's latest weapons, especially Sam Walker and Jack Hays.

Hays was a brand-new captain in the Rangers, but even before that he had taken as much of an interest in the Colt pistol as a cavalry weapon as Sam Walker had, and between the two of them they had convinced Mirabeau Lamar, the president of Texas, to send Walker east to purchase some more of Colt's Paterson Models— with revisions. Colt and Walker had met and discussed some possible revisions on the Paterson and nine months later here I was picking up the shipment.

The fact that the Paterson Model could easily scare the bejesus out of any intruder on the Texas frontier, be it Indian, Mexican or whoever, was a positive factor. Any man who can stand alone against a half dozen redskins is more than likely a bit touched to begin with, but with that Colt he'd sure as hell have those marauders' respect by the time he went under. That element of surprise and firepower was one thing, but the simple truth of the matter was that the Paterson wasn't the best put together gun to come along. And reloading could be a real chore, so that a man might find himself in a tight spot after using all his loads unless he had a spare weapon with him and someone else to load for him. So Walker had taken all of the complaints we had about the pistol and made a few suggestions to Colt about them. Sam had let me test-fire the new Paterson when I first got there and I had to admit it was a lot better gun than the old model.

Sam called it the Number 5 Model. It was over thirteen inches long with a seven-inch octagonal barrel and weighed just a tad more than the original model. The cylinders had been back-rounded, making it easier to place the percussion caps, and the butt of the handle had been rounded as well, making it fit better to the palm of the hand. And that was fine. But there were two other improvements that I had a lot more interest in, as would the rest of the Rangers who would use these weapons. The first was the new loading lever Sam had spoken of. It was a new addition to the pistol and would make loading much quicker, much easier. The second, and most important as far as a lot of us were concerned, was the new caliber of the weapon. Most of the originals had been in .34 or .36 calibers, which were far lighter than those used in the muskets and Hawkens we were used to. This Number 5 Model was bored for a .47 caliber round, which was the kind of slug that would at least guarantee your target would go down when you hit him, if not outright kill him. I had seen how a .45 or .54 Hawken round could destroy the meat of about any game it entered, so a .47 caliber hand gun ought to be able to do the same to a human.

And it fired six shots instead of five.

But that wasn't all I had. The year before, 1839, Sam Colt had brought out a line of long guns that had become fairly popular. The Model 39 Carbine or Shotgun, take your pick, was built to operate on the same method as Colt's pistols. They were single action and six shot. The carbines had loading levers, but the shotgun had to be broken down to load. They came in calibers ranging from .34 to .62, and for the fifty carbines I had, the ammunition would be the same as that of the pistols, a .47 caliber load. The carbine loads could have been larger, but it only made common sense to carry the same ammunition for one weapon as the other lest you ran out of lead for one of the guns or it didn't function right. Some might think it a comfort to have a big .62, but for my money it didn't always make a difference about a gun's size. When you ran out of ammunition or powder or the weapon went bad on you, it was about as useless as buffalo chips mixed in with a plate of greens.

The trails in that neck of the woods were a whole lot hillier than anything we had in Texas, and a lot greener, too. But I had a hunch that was where the similarity stopped. More trails were being opened up and more transportation was being developed for travelers heading to only God knew where. One thing about this country, no matter whether it was the eastern seaboard or your favorite spot west of the Mississippi, it was a sprawling land. And no matter where you went there always seemed to be people going somewhere. They headed south to the plantations; north and north by west to the fur trading regions of the mountain men as the trade began to die out; and just plain west trying to make a new start or escape debtors' prison or a wanted poster or a hundred other reasons. There were even a few who came back east, convinced that the civilization they left offered more than they could find or didn't want to handle out west. Yesiree, this country was full of people just atraveling.

Along the seaboard some cities had begun stringing rails and trying to make use of what they called steam engines and locomotives and such. I remembered one old-timer on the plains who had been back east and rid in one of them, claiming they put out an awful lot of soot and not much speed. An "Iron Horse," he said they called it.

"Better off riding that grulla of your'n or any other bronc," he added, shaking his head in despair. "Least-ways, you can get a hoss to go where you wants. This Iron Horse only goes where the rails is laid and that's sad, boy, that's sad."

The stagecoach was another means of travel that seemed to be catching on, and like it or not, it was the cause of a whole new career for those who had run afoul of the law. Highway robbery was the fancy back-east word they used for those who held up a stagecoach and robbed the passengers of their valuables. And the way people complained about it in the east, a body might figure they actually tolerated it. I reckon we just had a different way of thinking out west. You did your job and helped out your neighbor in the hard times and he would do the same for you. But if a man was too lazy to do for himself and decided to take something that wasn't rightly his to begin with, well, 'most any rancher, farmer, or merchant would tell you he had just flat worked too hard at making a go of it to consider thievery anything less than a killing offense. And you can believe that it only took a couple of dead corpses to make an honest man out of those who were planning that way of life out where I lived.

But I wasn't on the plains yet and that meant I had to be on the lookout for anybody or anything that was out of the ordinary, for word had it that these highwaymen weren't partial to stagecoaches alone. And a man alone would be an easier target to hit, so I had to be that much more cautious my own self.

At first I thought it was my imagination going to work on me because of my thoughts about the highwaymen. But after a while I knew it was that feeling a man gets when there is trouble about. You know it's out there and it's just waiting to happen, and somehow, like it or not, when it strikes out, it will be right where you happen to be sitting when it does. There is only one way to deal with it and that is to be ready all of the time. And after I held up a couple of times and checked my leaders, I knew that I had at least one advantage. I knew which direction this trouble was coming from.

I spotted them the first time while I was getting a drink from the water barrel. I was on a flat stretch of road and they were a mile or so back. There were two, maybe three, of them, and they did a right good job of getting out of sight when they came into view. It wasn't until noon of the second day that I took notice of them again in almost the same manner. And, once again, they pulled out of sight real quick-like.

That set me to wondering the rest of the afternoon. Were they the highwaymen I was thinking of or just travelers who liked to mind their own business and kept their distance? Hardly. I still had that gut feeling that told me they, whoever they were, were not to be trusted. Then it crossed my mind that perhaps I was being trailed for the shipment of guns I carried rather than any money I might have. Sam Colt's weapons had taken on a following of sorts and in times like these it did not seem that unreasonable that a man might kill for them, particularly if he could get more than one in the process. With that in mind, I didn't stop to make camp that night until I had found a grove of trees that would afford me as much cover as whoever it was following me. It's not that I didn't trust them, you understand, it's just that I didn't trust them.

When I set up camp that night it was all deliberate, so that they could see what I was doing until the fires died down and I turned in. Except I didn't do that. At the risk of making a mess of some of Colt's repeater rifles, I slid a box out and placed it not too far from the campfire, throwing my blanket over it as well as my hat. Then I sat off to one side of the fire and waited to see what the evening would bring. In those days you learned patience early in life or you might not survive. Mostly you developed it as a youngster when your pa or whoever took you out and taught you to hunt. When Pa was teaching me, one of the lessons he made clear was that depending on what type of game you were hunting, you didn't always have to track it down. "There will be times when you'll find yourself better off waiting for the game to come to you," he had said, and it was something I had not forgotten. I never did ask him if he was talking only of the four-legged game a man hunts or if it might apply as well to others, but I knew that in more than one case it had stood me well to remember that piece of wisdom when I was facing down the

warring renegades of the plains, both Indian and Mexican.
A man has to depend on every resource and instinct he
has to make a go of it in this land, and it was the early
lessons like that which gave you a whole new appreciation for not having your scalp hanging on some young
buck's coup stick.

I had a feeling that these birds following me had only
developed the patience of a buzzard, who waits only
until his prey is in an easy position to be taken before
he will attack. And I was right, for it was a good half
hour after sundown when they entered my camp. There
were two of them. They did not look particularly big or
mean, but they sure did appear to know their trade.
They entered from the west side and the only thought I
had was that they had circled the camp in order to
surprise me. They stood side by side for a second, then
each took a step to his off side and began to move in a
slow circle, all the time pointing their two-each horse
pistols at what was supposed to be me next to the fire.
Now, there ain't nothing that rattles a man more than
having the tables turned on him, especially when he
figures he's got a winning hand and can't do no wrong.
And that suited me fine.

"I'll call, boys," I said, cocking the Colt in my hand
and sticking the barrel out just far enough for them to
see without exposing myself. It caught them by surprise
and after a quick glance at the gun barrel and the figure
that was supposed to be me on the ground, they kind of
froze. "Now, lest you want to die without knowing
who it was done you in, you'd do well to lower the
hammers on them pistols and set 'em down right
gentle-like."

They did as they were told, but I thought I saw the
one on the far side of camp hesitate just a moment.

That was when I noticed the knives they each had stuck in their belts, and it struck me that they might be gamier than they looked. It also bothered me that they didn't seem as scared as a man should who has been caught unawares and is dealing with the business end of a gun, no matter what kind it is. I was out in the open now, and it was about then I felt a hard piece of metal stuck into my back about where my spine was and I knew I was playing a crooked game. Like I said, there ain't nothing rattles a man more'n being took by surprise.

"The game is over, my friend," the voice behind me said, and I could tell he was smiling just from the sound of him. I thought his voice had a trace of French in it the way he talked, but I was more interested in the gun he pushed a little harder into the small of my back. "Whether or not you want to lose big or little all depends on you," he said, as the others picked up their guns. It didn't take a fool to know what he was talking about, and I lowered the hammer on my own pistol and laid it down on the blanket-covered box of repeater rifles.

The first two kept a gun each trained on me while the one in back tossed away my bowie and began running a hand over my side and waist, probably looking for a money belt or whatever funds I had. I had the feeling he was going to be awful disappointed with what he found. But he never got that far, for that was when all hell broke loose!

A huge boom came from my left and the cannonlike effect surprised all of us, but none more than the man across the fire from me as he caught a slug high in the chest and fell over like one of those paper targets on a rifle range. It could have been St. Peter who fired that shot for all I cared. I at least had a fighting chance now as I spun around, bringing one hand down on the pistol held in my back as the man pulled the trigger. The gun went off and a burst of flame shot out of the barrel toward the ground, the bullet ricocheting into the air somewhere as I completed my turn by knocking him off-balance. Like a lot of those Frenchmen, this one was tall and skinny and one handful of his shirt was all I needed to bring him forward as I stuck out a foot, tripped him, and watched him fall into the dying fire. The heat was enough to bring him springing right back and I hit him twice, full in the face. I figured if I didn't break his jaw I had at least jarred loose a couple of teeth as he fell unconscious to the ground.

I would have paid more attention to the second man across the fire, but at the same time I was dealing with the third man, the other seemed to be fighting a losing battle. As soon as that shot rang out, the woman who had caused the ruckus back in New York stepped into the clearing, a pistol of her own in her hand, and started to say, "Drop it." The man simply brought the force of his own weapon down on the woman's hand, then shoved her aside as he made way to the clearing and escape. He must have heard the man behind him before he saw him, for that was when the drunken sergeant brought his musket down on the arm holding the pistol. It was an army-issue type that was easily heavy enough to break the man's arm. Then both men were without weapons and the big sergeant tackled the intruder, a heavyset, short man who never made it out of the clearing. By the time I had retrieved my own gun and knife, the soldier was sitting on the man's chest, slowly but efficiently beating his face to a pulp. There was blood all over his fist and it was hard telling whether it was his own or that of the man he sat on. I grabbed hold of his hand with my own the next time he brought it up. His only reaction was an angry look that questioned my authority to stop him.

"I don't think he's gonna hurt you anymore," I said evenly.

"Listen, bud. Anybody that shoves around my wife the way he—" He stopped then, as though letting out a secret. So that was it, I thought. That was the connection between the two. The woman, meanwhile, had brushed herself off and was rubbing her shoulder where the man had hit her. She didn't seem a bit upset about what was being said or done, not at all.

"He may be worth more to you alive than dead," I said. The anger faded from his face now as I let go of his wrist, replaced by a look of curiosity. "There might be a reward on these ruffians," I continued. "Pay a visit to the constable in the next town and they might pay for turning 'em in."

Apparently he was the kind of man who would forget anything if the price was right, for he got off the man and began brushing himself off as well. I could tell by the look in his eyes that he was envisioning some kind of reward money in the not-too-distant future. Both of the outlaws we had fought were out cold and the one who had been shot was probably dead before he hit the ground, the bullet striking him right above the breastbone, so I put away my six-shooter and studied the two while he wiped the blood from his hand.

The immediate difference in them from the last time I had seen them was that he no longer wore an army uniform and she had on a man's shirt and trousers instead of the fancy waitress outfit. You could dress some women in a man's clothes and they would look no different from a scrawny kid working his way west or, in the case of some of the older ones, a man who'd fought a griz for his hibernation supplies and lost. But not this one. She was like Ellie in that respect. No matter how big a man's shirt you put on her, you just couldn't hide her . . . femaleness. If you know what I mean.

And her husband, if that was what he was, would need a hell of a lot more than a change of clothes to make a sight of difference in him. He was still a big, ugly brute, as obstinate as he had been the first time I met him. What I noticed now was that even stone-cold sober, the man had a fire in him that would be hard to put out once he got whatever it was that kept it going into his mind. Me, I was betting it was the woman every time.

"I'm Nate Callahan," I said, sticking a paw out when he had finished caring for his hand.

"Joe Ward," he said, not bothering to shake hands. "And, like you heard, this is my wife, Charlotte." He nodded briefly to her.

"A pleasure, I'm sure," the woman said. She wasn't shy at all about shaking my hand and I could tell from her tone of voice that it had the same sound as when I'd seen her last. Her smile was what Sam or Finn would have called charming, but I had an idea that behind it was a knowledge that she had just run into someone who could give her the attention she wanted. And just thinking that was enough to make my palms sweat.

"You say they're worth money?" Ward asked, but the greed had gone out of his eyes and I had a feeling he was saying it just to keep the woman from making more trouble.

"That's what I heard on the way up. Seems there was a fair amount of robbery going on and rewards were put out on some of these birds." The conversation seemed to dry up about then and we all of us went about disposing of the outlaws as if we knew what had to be done. I had an old blanket in the back of the wagon and we rolled the dead man in it, tying up the other two as they gained consciousness. Neither of them would be much trouble from here on out, the tall skinny one more worried about his loose teeth and dislocated jaw than anything else, and the man Ward had taken on had been reduced to a whimpering coward.

"You can camp here overnight," I said when we were through. "Unless I'm mistaken, there's a town not too far ahead and we can drop these birds off tomorrow."

Both nodded silently, which I took to mean they had accepted my offer. I gathered more wood to rekindle the fire and they brought their own equipment up to the camp, two horses and a pack mule. The mule was a piebald and when I saw it I knew that it had been these two who had been trailing me for the past day or two. Still, they had saved my life, and a man didn't turn away a person who had done that, even a stranger.

But when I turned in that night, even after the evening's events, I still had that feeling in my gut that trouble was about.

Chapter Three

It wasn't until we had broken camp and been on the trail for the better part of an hour that I thought to ask Ward what he was doing out of uniform. In the excitement of last night's events, I had noticed the lack of uniform on the man but had forgotten to ask why he wasn't wearing it, realizing now that it was one of the reasons I felt uneasy about the man.

"Let's just say I give it up," Ward said, more nervous than shy about making the statement. "Besides," he added, looking at his wife, "Lotty wasn't too stuck on army life, anyway."

I thought I saw the same twinge of nervousness in the woman as she smiled weakly to confirm her husband's statement. Gone was the flirty way of acting she had put on the night before. Ever since we had broken camp she had been the perfect picture of a timid, obedient wife. But right along with it shone through the fear of a woman who was fighting to control her sanity. Something was wrong, but it was their life and I wasn't about to meddle in it.

"Enlistment up?" I asked after we'd gone a fair ways in silence again.

"Yeah. Yeah, it's up." The man was getting riled now. The look on his face said it wasn't any of my business and when he pulled alongside the Conestoga and grabbed ahold of my arm, I knew that was just what he was going to say. I pulled the wagon to a halt and jerked my arm free.

"It ever cross your mind, Callahan, that you're just a mite too nosey for your own good?" he said through grit teeth.

"Well, now, friend, I'll tell you," I said in as even a voice as I could manage. I wasn't used to being pushed without pushing back hard my own self, but at the same time I could understand how the man must have felt. "Any other time, I wouldn't be as curious about you or anyone else riding with me, but with what I've got back there," I said, throwing a thumb over my shoulder at the contents of the Conestoga, "well, it's a big responsibility, and I'm just not looking forward to any more run-ins like last night."

"Mister, I saved your life last night! You think I give a damn about your lousy wagon!"

"I'm thinking if you didn't you wouldn't have been following me for two days like you did," I replied, my own voice getting hard now.

"We don't mean you any harm," the woman said, not sounding shy at all now. "It's just that Joe's . . . cautious. Yes, Joe's cautious, Mr. Callahan."

For all I knew they could have been partners with the three who had tried to hold me up last night and, getting greedy, decided that one less partner made the pot that much bigger. For all I knew, they might cut loose the bonds on the prisoners we now had and still take what I had. I hadn't mentioned what kind of cargo I was carrying, for there had always been a need for more weapons on the frontier, and some men simply did not care how or where they got them. They were that precious a commodity. The greedy look on Ward's face the night before told me that even if he was being honest with me, the man was not beyond doing something a bit shady to make an extra dollar.

I let the subject drop right there and let out a few cuss words just to let my team know it was time to be moving on. Ward must have been willing to do the same, for he said nothing more the rest of the morning.

I tried concentrating on the trail, but in the back of my mind something said that there was still enough to be suspicious about my two companions to warrant an extra glance their way once in a while. Ward had sounded convincing enough and I might have believed him were it not for what the woman had said. Or maybe it was the way she'd said it, as though she did not know the full story and was put in the position of making up bits and pieces as her husband unveiled the puzzle. That they meant me no harm was a possibility I had to admit. But Ward a cautious man? My eye and Betty Martin! It didn't take long to see that Joe Ward worked as hard at his off-duty drinking as he did at his soldiering, or whatever his true profession was. And the way he had come charging into camp in the face of two loaded guns the night before did not sound any too cautious, either. A cautious man would have had an extra weapon with him and shot as many of his adversaries as possible before doing anything as reckless as Joe Ward had done. No, the man was far from cautious. In fact, he seemed to relish such danger, if the look on his face while he was beating that one ruffian to a pulp was any indication. When he had come charging into camp, I thought I had caught a glimpse of madness in his eye that was reminiscent of what I had seen in Lije Harper, Ellie's pa. It was the kind of look that made you keep your wits about you even when the man was acting normal, for you could never tell when that devilish look would appear again. It was all part of the uneasy feeling I had about these two, and no matter how hard I tried I just couldn't shake it.

Along about noon we came on a town that looked big enough to get rid of the thugs who had tried to do me in. The frontier was still wide and wild enough where only the larger cities and towns that functioned as county seats could afford to pay a full-time lawman. Many of the smaller towns had a part-time constable or city marshal to fend for them for little or no salary. And it was generally recognized that once a man was outside the city limits, he became his own law, especially in the wilder parts of the country. A man's principles carried a lot of weight on the frontier, but more often than not their strength depended on how much firepower the man had to back up his play. So you might say I was relieved to see a town this size, feeling that much better when I pulled the wagon and prisoners up in front of the local jail.

The sheriff put the prisoners in one of his cells and sent a young boy across the street for the doctor once he saw the face of Ward's victim. The doctor turned out to be a crotchety old man of sixty who acted as though the whole of us were right gamey for interrupting him the way we had. But he had a sense of humor, I'll say that for him. After he got through with the man in the cell, he asked to take a look at the body of the dead man, for what I figured must have been the official coroner's report. Ward and me unloaded the blanket-wrapped body as the sheriff looked on. The man was as rock-hard as any mesa I'd ever traveled over and was dead as could be, but I reckon the doctor and sheriff had to follow whatever their procedure was and examine the man anyway.

"When was this man shot?" the doctor asked, taking a look at the huge bullet hole in the man's chest, then turning the body partially over to examine the gaping hole in the back.

"Last night," Ward said.

"Well, if he wasn't dead then, he sure as hell is now," the doctor said with a straight face. Then, looking up at the lawman from his kneeling position, he added, "Just for the report, George, you can say this man met his death at the hands of a damn good shot."

I was right about the two in the jail being highwaymen, as well as the dead man. All three were worth forty dollars each, but the sheriff decided he was only going to give Ward the reward money for two of them.

"What!" Ward yelled, his face slowly turning beet-red. "I brought in three of them. What do you mean you ain't paying for three of them?"

"Oh, you brought in three of them, mister," the sheriff said, still calm as could be. "But you've got to admit, that one fella in there hasn't got enough of a face left to believe what he used to look like even if *he* was to tell me."

I had no interest in the reward money, only in getting back to Texas with my cache of weapons, so I didn't say much when Ward laid claim to taking care of the three outlaws all by himself. When he pocketed his money he seemed to disappear, for I had no idea where he went, although a good bet would have been the nearest bar. Me, I headed for what looked like a general store. The blanket that dead man had been wrapped in was beyond use and would have to be replaced. It didn't seem worth starting out again, so I figured to stay overnight and then get an early start in the morning.

I was going through a stack of blankets, trying to find something that was serviceable, when she walked up beside me. She could have been any woman doing her shopping as far as the owner was concerned, but I got that feeling she was going to make more of it than it was or should be.

"You're quite the businessman, aren't you?"

"Ma'am?"

"Lotty," she said, placing a hand on my arm. "Please call me Lotty. All my friends do." She placed some emphasis on that last piece, saying it just loud enough for anyone else who might want to gossip about it to hear.

"Lotty." I said it more by way of acknowledgment than anything else, not even taking notice of her. It must have had some effect on her, for when she spoke her voice had grown a bit harder than I was used to hearing.

"What I meant was you're a very cold, calculating man . . . wouldn't you say?"

"That's what I've been told," I said, looking at her just as hard as I was speaking. "You see, Lotty, I was brought up to believe that you did all your work till it was done and then you played if you'd a mind to."

"And you don't choose to play?"

"Well, ma'am," I said, pushing my hat back, "it's like this. You see, ever since I struck out on my own, well, it's just been one damn thing after another, and I surely don't recall ever having the need for funning once I got used to working from can-see to can't-see. I purely don't."

I wasn't about to tell her about the times I'd had with Ellie since we had married, for it would have done nothing but make her madder than she already was. There was no denying that Lotty Ward was one beautiful woman. She was tall for a woman, her black hair and eyes reminding me of the pretty young Mexican women a man could find in the marketplace or square of almost any village, large or small. To hear Finn talk, they had some sort of Castilian beauty that made them one notch better than the rest. Something to do with their bloodline, I reckon. But to me pretty was pretty, and the only thing richer bloodlines did for a woman was make her blush that much redder. The thing about Lotty Ward was that, beautiful as she was, she could never hold a candle to Ellie or how I felt about her. She had been right about me being cold and hard, for when there was something to be done, I would just as soon get it over with as put it off. And there was only one woman who had ever been able to stir up my feelings and that was Ellie.

She must have taken what I said as a flat denial of whatever it was she had in mind, for she drifted off to a small section of home and women's things while I finished my own looking. When I paid for my blanket, I left the store and took a seat outside on the boardwalk, thinking I might see Ward and where he was coming from before he came searching out me and his wife. One thing was certain; if he found me anywhere near his wife after he had had a few drinks, I could count on that wild look coming to his eye again. And at the moment I wasn't looking for any more excitement than I had to have.

"I suppose I should apologize," she said, taking a seat next to me. She was back to being formal again, which was fine with me. I would still have to watch what I was saying. Like I said, I do better dealing with a man than I do a woman. Man will tell you right off what's on his mind, but a woman will play games with you just to see what you're about. At least that was the impression I had of this woman.

"I knew a fella back on the plains some time ago," I said, still looking across the street for Ward. "Had himself a line of thought, he did. Said most people know what they have to do. They just ask other people for advice so's when it goes wrong they can blame it on them." I paused a moment, then looked at her. " 'Course, they never give the other person much credit for their decision if it pans out in their favor, you understand. No, ma'am." Then I propped the chair back against the wall and pulled my hat down just far enough to see past the rim. "You do and say what you like, Mrs. Ward. Most people do, whether it gets them in trouble or not."

She was silent for a while before I heard her say, "Please call me Lotty," which I reckon was supposed to be her way of apologizing. I couldn't see her face but she sure did sound sincere, and it crossed my mind that this woman was about as changeable as a Texas skyline. I had seen storm clouds on the horizon some days that took the better part of the afternoon to get anywhere close to us and never did nothing. And then there were those days when it seemed like it couldn't be better and within five minutes all hell would break loose in the form of a norther or a hidden rain cloud you never saw or any other number of things. I had heard more than one man refer to the weather as being as fickle as a

woman, and at the moment I couldn't think of any other
way to describe this woman than that Texas weather—
changeable, downright changeable.

"That husband of yours," I said, pushing my hat
back again and facing her. "Did he really get out of the
army, like he says?"

"I don't know, Mr. Callahan. I honestly don't know."
The tone of her voice and the look on her face were of
pure puzzlement and I had the feeling that right now
she was telling the truth. "The day after the incident in
the restaurant he came by and told me his enlistment
was up and to start packing, that he was going to head
west. So I naturally assumed—"

"No explanation? Nothing? You didn't even ask him?"

"I'm afraid you don't understand, Mr. Callahan,"
she said hesitantly. She bit her lip before speaking, then
said it all, as if to get it over with and out of the way.
"My husband is a consummate professional at his work.
So, you see, you *don't* ask any questions of Sergeant
Joseph Ward, nor do you *tell* him what to do. You
simply follow his orders, or—" She stopped then and I
was sure that if she had stayed I would have heard the
sobs that went along with the tears that welled up in her
eyes as she spoke. But she was gone then, walking
quickly down the boardwalk the way a woman will
when she only has a few minutes to get to the store
before it closes for the day.

Watching her go, I suddenly knew why she was such
a hard person to figure out. It wasn't that she was
changeable as much as that she was mixed up and hurt.
Her eyes had been filled with fear and pain before she
had finished speaking, before the tears came. It was the
kind of look that a body doesn't forget easy. You see it
in the eyes of the first rabbit you snare and think you

can tame. You keep it caged up and every time you look at it you see that same painful look in its eyes. And, finally, when you figure it ain't going to stay locked up, when you know it was meant to be free in the wilds, you go to let it out and find that it's too late, for it's dead. It was that kind of look she had.

As for Sergeant Joseph Ward, I had seen his likes before. Men who bullied and pushed to get their way, believing that the use of violence and fighting was the only way to settle anything, and that included any home life they had. And that usually wasn't much. The first time I had run into him I could see he was a jealous man, and the more I saw of him the more I knew that drunk or sober, the man didn't want to share any part of his wife with anyone else. He was the kind of man who would never trust her to do anything by her own self, wouldn't let her do anything unless it was with his consent, and then would probably watch to make sure she did it alone.

Maybe that was why she taunted him the way she did. Why she made advances toward other men. It was probably her way of getting back at him. It didn't make an awful lot of sense to push a person like Ward, knowing he would only torment you for it, but then I reckon that if dishing out torment becomes a way of life, well, desperate people do desperate things. If a body thought about it, it was kind of sad in a way. I remembered Finn always talking about those storybook characters he was reading about and how there were men who became legends in their own time. Me, I had my own thoughts on people like that. It seemed that wherever you went, people always had some legend they were talking about, somebody who was a hero and all. Trouble was none of them was ever alive that they was talking about, so I just figured any man who became a legend in his own time sure didn't live too awful long. And if what I had just heard was right, well, I had a hunch that maybe desperate people, the ones like Lotty and Joe Ward, had the same fate as those living legends. For the kind of life they led, it sure didn't seem like they'd live too awful long.

Ward had not set out to find the nearest bar at all. When he returned he had a couple of shiny double eagles to show for it. As it turned out, he didn't have a hell of a conscience about those three birds that tried to do me in, for he had sold not only their horses but their gear as well. Either the sheriff didn't mind or Ward hadn't told him about their possessions to begin with. The most amazing thing of all was that the man was still sober!

After Lotty had left in tears, I had headed back for my wagon, spending the rest of the afternoon cleaning Colt's new Model 5 and explaining just how it worked to some interested townfolks. For some reason or other Joe Ward seemed happier than I had ever seen him before, probably from his newfound pocket money, I thought. When he asked about Lotty, I told him I hadn't seen her in a few hours, but he didn't show much concern over her.

"She's probably out looking for fancies," was all he said, a smile still on his face. "You know how women are."

"I reckon." I shrugged and continued to put back together my Number 5 Model and load it. I had a feeling that when Ward found his wife she would be sitting in some corner crying her eyes out rather than window shopping. Besides, the plain fact of the matter was that I *didn't* know how women were, whatever the hell that meant. I was just a man trying to make his way on the frontier, and learning how to stay alive and keep that way was enough of a chore for anybody. Truth be known, I didn't really mind it at all. But try and figure out how "women are"? Hell, I had made up my mind a long time back that if a man sat and pondered on women and the things they do and why they do it, why, his head would explode from all the things he'd find out! I had the same feeling about Finn, never could understand how he could read all them books and find room in his head to remember them all. The whole of it was just a pure puzzlement. That it was.

"Tell you what, Callahan," he said, slapping me on the shoulder in what was supposed to be a friendly gesture, "you finish your ordnance there and I'll go find her and we'll get us some supper. I found a place down the street that claims to serve a healthy meal for fifty cents. And I'll pay."

He said nothing else and left.

The prospect of something besides hot coffee, hardtack and a slice of jerked beef for a meal was welcome indeed, for a man tends to tire of his own cooking on the trail. And if Ward wanted to pay for it, so much the better, for I was down to my last few dollars. Most eateries put out a full-course meal for all of fifteen cents and if this place Ward had located was charging three times that much, then it ought to be decent at that.

I wouldn't have paid much attention to them if it hadn't been for the dark-blue uniforms they wore and the fact that there were a half dozen of them. They came riding from the east side of town and they were sure enough soldiers. Nothing like the garrison troops I had seen back in New York, though. These men had on work uniforms and had been traveling some and you'd not find any fancy trappings on them. The leader, an officer of some sort, dismounted in front of the saloon and gave orders to one of the others who led the horses away while the rest entered the saloon.

A short time later the Wards approached the wagon. He didn't say where he had found his wife and I didn't ask, but she appeared to have regained her composure, for other than a few red lines at the corners of her eyes I couldn't tell she had been crying. Ward led us off to the eating place he had found and once again the conversation kind of dried up.

Whoever built the establishment knew what he had in mind. It was put together to stay and although it didn't have a second floor, just looking at it gave a body the feeling that he could eat his meal without having to worry about the roof caving in from too much rain or snow. A sod hut was fine for a temporary structure, but unless you built it into the side of a good-sized hill your roof might be less than sturdy when bad weather came.

The lady who owned and ran the place was a fat, jovial person. You could tell right off that she loved cooking and enjoyed seeing people eat. She seated us at one of the three community tables in the place and rattled off what she had available rather than handing out a menu. Not that I would expect anything like that when I got this far out into the wilderness. Once you got away from the city, people were pretty simple about their wants and needs and tended to treat everyone the same, whether they wore work clothes or fancy Sunday-go-to-meeting dress-ups.

"I'll take some of that beef, as long as you cook it inside and out," I said when she asked for my order.

"Oh?" She cocked her head to one side and I thought I caught a trace of Irish as she looked at me curiously.

"Yes, ma'am. You see, I just come from New York, where a friend took me out to one of them fancified eateries. And I'll tell you, ma'am, I ordered a steak well-done, but when I cut into it . . . why, I've seen animals hurt worse than that that got well! Besides, I've had my share of raw meat and the only reason I liked it then was because it was all I had to eat."

"So you'd ruther make sure it's dead before you eat it," she said with a laugh. I might have exaggerated some on what I just said, but I couldn't brag too much on how those back-east cooks pan-fried a steak, that was for sure.

"Same here," Ward said.

"Yes, please," Lotty said, with a smile that gave me the notion she was remembering her own days as a waitress.

The coffee was near scalding hot and the food was worth waiting for. We were served plates of steaming beef that were thick-cut and burned just right. When I tasted the homemade biscuits she set out I figured the meal was worth every bit of the price, for I'd not tasted anything so good since leaving Ellie. I was so busy putting away that food that I forgot about asking Ward if he had seen the soldiers riding into town. I didn't think about it again until the six of them entered the eatery. All I needed was a quick glance at them and the slow frown that began to form on Ward's face to know that there was more brewing here than just food.

"Friends of yours?" I asked, trying to sound casual as I took another sip of coffee.

"Not exactly." Ward was acting the same way,

waiting to see if they would make the first move or if they'd come to eat.

Our table was against the back wall. Not that I minded at all, for at least with your back to a wall you know where the other fellow's coming from, and when the young officer passed right on by Fanny, as the lady running the place called herself, without so much as a howdy-do, I knew they were here on business. I cussed some to myself. Damn, but I hated being interrupted.

"The captain wants to see you, Sergeant Ward," the young kid said when he got to our table. He was standing in front of Ward and I saw that he couldn't have been but maybe twenty if he was lucky. I wasn't about to jump into something when I had no idea of what was going on, so I waited for Ward's reply. Out of the corner of my eye, it looked like he was starting to enjoy himself.

"Lieutenant, we're more'n a hundred miles out of New York," he said, a mischievous smile coming to his face. "Now, you don't seriously think I'm traveling that kind of distance just to see that old fool." When the lieutenant's face flushed at the audacity of what the man had said to him, Ward continued. "Look, sir, you and your boys there have a seat and I'll buy you supper, okay? Fanny, here, she puts out a right tasty meal. So why not—"

"The captain said he wants to see you, Sergeant," the young buck said, trying his best to sound tough and old. I do believe he even tried to grit his teeth when he said it, he was trying that hard.

"You bite down much harder, son, and you'll bust off the top of your teeth," I said, keeping from smiling as best I could. "Knew a fellow did just that one time. Said it was god-awful painful."

"And just what business of this is yours?" the kid asked, coming to a full flush of red now that he saw Ward was widening his smile over what I had said. The lad hadn't been too awful successful at whatever his mission was so far, and feeling like a fool never did a hell of a lot for any man's temper, young or old.

"Well, now, it's probably none of my business if I get real thoughtful about it. On the other hand, the wind you two are creating jabbering away like you are is just flat making my food cold." I shrugged. "Why not take the man up on his offer and have a seat? Or leave." I said the last part hard so he'd know that if it wasn't my business, I was making it mine. Ma taught us manners, making sure we knew how to make people welcome wherever we went. And I was trying, I honest to God was. But this fella was trying to throw his weight around where he didn't have none to throw and I was getting a mite testy about it.

"Don't get smart with me, mister!" he said, nearly yelling as an arm shot out and he pointed a long, bony finger across the table at me. Now, I don't like people pointing at me. Fingers, guns, nothing. Ma said it was a lack of manners, and if anyone knew manners, it was Ma. "This is government business and none of your affair, so if you want to eat, just take your plate outside. But don't butt in here, understand?" His face was livid and he had the look of a man who was ready to fight.

I didn't say a word. There was an awful lot of silence while the rest of them waited to see what I would do. I looked down at my half-empty plate of cold beef and that tore it! Without looking up I slowly pulled the napkin from my shirt and set it in my lap, probably looking like I was going to take the man up on his order. If he saw the red creeping up my neck, he didn't

notice it or take it as a warning, and that suited me fine. **Because** when I looked up at him and his friends, my hand came up, too, and in it was the Model 5 Colt, pointed straight at his belly.

"Sonny, I've done my damnedest to be accommodating with you, but I've about had it!" It wasn't the tone of my voice as much as the sight of that gun barrel that made his face turn sheet-white. "Now, whatever you and Ward have got to palaver about may be government or personal or whatever you want to call it, but it can wait. You see, I don't get a chance at eating meals like this too often, and when some *pilgrim* takes it on himself to come between me and my food, well, it makes me downright edgy. And in your case, sonny, if you keep apushing it"—I cocked the Colt, the sound of it filling the room—"it could be real unhealthful for you." I said it all hard and even, and there wasn't a bit of bluff to it. I hadn't shot anyone over a meal, but I knew of one man who got so riled about a similar incident that he put a new belly button right where one fella's nose used to be.

"You know he's right, Lieutenant." The voice spoke at the same time I heard another pistol being cocked at the side of the room. It was Fanny. With both hands she held one of those oversized horse pistols that give a man the feeling that even if the ball was to miss him at such close range, the concussion of the blast would likely blind him or kill him. At the sound of a second pistol being cocked one of the lieutenant's compadres must have gotten nervous, for he was snaking his hand to his side when Fanny spoke again, directing her aim at him now. "Tut, tut, lad," she said in as calm a voice as I'd ever heard a woman speak in who was facing possible danger. "Jocko taught me well, he did." A

frown came to the faces of the troopers and the lieutenant and I knew good and well all they figured this
woman knew about was the cooking of meals. But
Fanny was educating them real fast and were I a betting
man I'd have put money on the fact that she saw the
same thing I did in these men. "Me late husband,
Jocko was," she added by way of explanation. "And
he taught me how to load and fire quite well.

"Now, as I was saying, Lieutenant, the young man
is most certainly right." She said it with a thick trace of
her Irish accent now and I had the feeling she was one
of those who had lived through the period when the
Irish in this country were considered no better off, and
often worse, than the luckless slaves. We were starting
to make a name for ourselves now, and one thing I had
noticed was that whenever an Irishman had the upper
hand he was sure to let you know what his true origins
were. "I'll welcome any man from any land in my
place, lad, but they all come to eat, not raise a ruckus.
So perhaps it would be best if you and yours simply
left." When the lieutenant gave her a look of contempt,
she added, "I'd have no trouble at all having George
Jacobs lock up the lot of you, if that's what you're
thinking." The young officer was turning red, feeling
like a fool again. At least he showed a little sense when
he made his next decision and left the eatery without a
word, glancing over his shoulder only once at Ward and
me as he did.

"Whew!" she said after they were gone. And for the
first time I saw sweat break out on her forehead as she
ran a hand across it. "Would you believe that is the
first time I've ever had to throw anyone out of my
place? But I said it, just like Jocko taught me."

I got up and took the pistol from her hand, slowly

uncocking it. Then I smiled at her and winked as I handed the weapon back to her. "You did fine, Fanny, just fine. And thanks."

She got us all another portion of beef, biscuits and coffee then and I finished the meal without another interruption. It struck me that Lotty had been real quiet during the whole affair while Ward had sat back and found it more amusing than anything. Whatever it was the young lieutenant and Ward had to settle didn't seem to bother the ex-sergeant too much, and if Lotty had any knowledge of it, she didn't show it. Other than that, I concentrated on the meal, figuring by the time we were through that I was good for at least three days on the trail.

"Where are you folks going?" I asked when we left. I was hoping they had some destination other than mine or that Ward had not gotten tired of being a civilian and wanted to go back east to his army and his stripes. Life would be a lot easier if they were not around to give me that uneasy feeling.

"Hadn't give it much thought," Ward replied. "Maybe I'll just wait until my money runs out. Got enough now to last a couple of months, even if I was to stay here. Right now I'm gonna get a drink." I think Lotty and me, the both of us, knew that it was near impossible for a man like Ward to stop at one drink. "Why don't I buy you one, Callahan?" He seemed friendly enough, but I knew that his type was the kind that got mean after he had had a few too many and I had no real interest in getting involved with his domestic life.

"No, thanks, Ward," I said. "I'd just as soon turn in and get an early start tomorrow. But you go ahead and have a good time."

"That's right, Joseph, you go ahead," Lotty said.

Then she looked at me in that way she had and said, "I'm going to take a walk before I go to bed." She was changing roles again, acting like she had before, and all I could think was she was, by God, trying to get us both killed by a jealous husband.

"On the other hand," I said, "maybe I could use a drink. But just one, Ward, just one."

Like I said, I've got no interest in getting involved in domestic quarrels.

Chapter Four

They were just starting to call them saloons back
then, getting the word from some fancy French term, if
what Finn said was right. Before that they were called
roadhouses and they did double duty as both a bar and
eatery. But these saloons, well, they were supposed to
be for drinking only, and for a friendly drink that
sounded right fine. The trouble was that after men like
Ward had some of those friendly drinks, they got downright hostile.

This saloon wasn't much different from Fanny's eatery.
It was only half the size, a long bar against one wall
that was as crudely made as the handful of tables and
chairs in the place. After I adjusted my eyes to the
dark, I saw we were getting some hard looks from the
other customers. At first I couldn't figure out why, then
I remembered that Lotty was with us and that women
were seldom seen in drinking establishments unless
they were bar maids. Not that a woman didn't take a
nip at home now and then. But drinking in public was
out of place and frowned upon.

We took a seat near the door and I could still feel the disapproving looks thrown our way as the bartender, a huge bear of a man with a drooping mustache, approached our table.

"What'll it be, folks?" he asked, not seeming to care whether we had a woman in our company or not.

"What have you got?" I said before Ward could blurt out an order for us.

"Well, we've got the usual house whiskey," he said, then paused, eyeing Lotty before he continued. "But maybe you'd like to try something new we've got on hand, ma'am. Lager beer, it's called. German-made, I hear, and right out of Cincinnati. 'Tain't harsh as the whiskey, and it's as close to a civilized woman's drink as you'll find in this area. I highly recommend it, ma'am."

"Thank you, sir," Lotty said with her best smile. "I do believe I'll take you up on your offer."

"Make it two of those beers," I said.

"Whiskey, mine," Ward said. "And leave the bottle."

When the man returned he had two mugs of a dark liquid, which I took to be the beer he had spoken of, and a bottle and glass on his tray. For as small a place as he had he sure put on a good show of making a body feel at home, I'll give him that.

"Are you sure you want the bottle?"

"Yup. Here, I'll pay you for it now," Ward said, digging into his pocket with one hand while he downed a shot of the liquid. When he swallowed, I thought I knew why the bartender had asked if he wanted the whole bottle. He half slammed the glass down, sat stock-still, frozen in place, and I'd have sworn he looked like a frog the way his eyes bugged out! They watered some and I fully expected him to snort fire out of his nose any second. Instead, he slowly turned his head to the barman, his voice hoarse when he spoke. "That's smooth," he managed to get out, followed by, "Where did you get this stuff?"

"Now you know why I asked if you wanted the whole bottle," the big man said, smiling. "Most people can't stand more'n a shot or two. Get it from the boys up in the hills every so often. Aged in the keg Busthead, they call it. Right potent, eh?"

"My God, what do they make it with?" Lotty asked, taking in the expression on her husband's face.

"Well, ma'am, nearest I can figure is they start out with a barrel of rainwater, throw in a goodly portion of grain alcohol, a plug of tobacco for color and a bar of lye soap to take the taste some. Good for what ails you, too, I hear."

"If you're a dying man, maybe," Lotty said, for the first time showing what appeared to be genuine concern for her husband's health.

"Look on the bright side, Lotty," I said, finding it hard to keep from smiling, "maybe it'll cure him of drinking."

But my remark had little effect on either of them, for Ward paid for the bottle and the drinks shortly, this time only sipping his whiskey. As it turned out, the beer was sort of tasty after all. Pa had introduced me to Irish rye whiskey and the ale served on the eastern seaboard in my youth, and I had tasted the tequila of Mexico and a few of the various home brews, but never anything with the taste of this new beer. It wasn't half-bad, and who could tell, maybe it would catch on, especially at a nickel a glass.

We drank in silence for a while, each of us nursing our own thoughts as well as our drinks. There were still some customers who were staring at us as if we'd go away if they did it long enough. And the more they kept at it, the more I had the uneasy feeling that we would get no kind of help from them if and when Ward started to get violent. His system must have been getting used to the whiskey, or whatever it was, for he was taking bigger gulps of it now. I couldn't tell what he was thinking, but it was plain to see he was getting moody, and the way Lotty was starting to give me those looks again it only made me feel that much more edgy.

I was thinking on how I could get out of that place before Ward caught on to what his wife was doing when they walked in. All six of them. Real quiet-like they passed us and went on to the back of the room, where they ordered drinks. And that was when I knew there was no leaving this saloon without looking like some kind of coward. Ma taught us to avoid fighting, that it was ungentlemanly, the same as most mothers will tell their boys. But it was Pa who took Finn and me out back of the barn not long after Ma's lecture and set us straight on the matter. "Your Ma's right about fighting, boys," he said, adding, "as far as she goes. If you can talk your way out of a fight, that's fine. But you listen careful, lads. When you *do* get into one, you make sure you win!" I had never forgotten what Pa said, which is why I automatically found myself looking for advantages to take hold of from where I was seated. They would come at us, that much I knew. And there would be no backing down by the young lieutenant, no being made a fool of again, or he would lose whatever respect his men had left for him.

I was seated with my back to the wall, so none would get me from behind. That left the sides to worry about. Lotty was seated to my left and Ward was right across

the table from me, his back to them. It must have been
the look on my face that made him ask what was wrong
as I saw the group rise from their table.

"Visitors," I said, not taking my eyes from them,
"again."

Ward glanced over his shoulder and when he looked
back he did not seem moody at all. He downed a fast
gulp of his whiskey as he said, "And I ain't feeling
hospitable at all." But looking at him, I knew he was
just talking empty words. The grin on his face and that
look in his eyes told me he wasn't mad at all. Hell, if
he was mad at what was about to take place, I was one
of them Franciscan monks! If anything, Ward was looking forward to our confrontation with this crew. And
that may have been the only good thing about the
situation, knowing that unless he got cold-cocked from
the rear, Ward was going to go down swinging.

I pushed my chair back some as they neared us,
giving me just enough room to not get caught empty-
handed. The only thing bothering me now was that I
had no idea what the other five would do. I had heard
the lieutenant and had him figured, but a man tends to
get cautious when he has no idea what his opponent
will do. The lieutenant was tall more than muscular, but
the others looked as though they could be real trouble.
The big one and another stopped between Lotty and
Ward, the big one eyeing her. The loudmouth officer
had taken up a position right behind Ward with a third
man, and the other two stood off to my right, but not
that far. They must have figured that me with my back
to the wall was going to be easy doings.

"I didn't know they had your kind of woman this far
out," the big one said, placing a rough hand on Lotty's
shoulder.

"Take your hand off of me." She said it hard, like she meant business, and it would be hard to blame her, as ugly as that fellow was.

"You heard her," Ward said when the man left his hand on her shoulder and Lotty winced as he squeezed hard.

At the same time the lieutenant reached down and grabbed Ward by the shirt, saying, "You're coming with me, Sergeant."

Ward gave a quick glance at his whiskey glass, then looked at me as he said, "Waste of good whiskey," and threw the contents in the loudmouth's face. The kid let out a yell as Ward pushed back his chair, throwing the man in back of him off-balance, and backhanded the ruffian at his wife's side. I hit the one closest to me with a roundhouse left that caught him square on the chin.

Now, there are little things a body notices after he's gotten used to them over the years, and when they all of a sudden change you get right edgy about it. What I felt was someone tugging my bowie from my left side, and I was damned if I was going to get hog stuck with my own knife! But I had no need to worry, for it was Lotty who had pulled my knife and now I saw her take a hard swing at the big man's wrist, saw blood flow freely over it as she made contact. The man quickly jumped back and I smiled at Lotty for showing him hot to start the ball. She had guts, she did.

That's when the second one hit me. I caught it right on the chin and fell back against the wall. He wasn't big but he was fast and of a sudden all I could feel was pain in my side as he hammered away at me. If I didn't stop him right quick I wasn't long for this world, which is when the pain turned to anger and I stepped on his foot with all my weight. He let out a yell and took one last swing at me, missing me but hitting the wall as I ducked. I sidestepped him, bringing my knee up into his gut as his motion carried him forward. He would have stood up but I yanked out that Colt and whacked him behind the ear and he fell to the floor.

I took a quick survey of the room. The customers had no wish for a part in our fight, some of them even cheering on the soldiers. One of them was flattened out on the floor near Ward as the ex-sergeant stood toe and toe with the lieutenant, slowly turning his face into raw meat with each swing of his fist. The man accompanying the big one who had taken to Lotty stood with his hands in the air as the barkeep stood behind him, his shotgun at the ready. The only one not yet out of commission was the ruffian I had hit first. He had his hand on the hilt of a boot knife when I leveled the Colt at him.

"Don't do it, son," I said, cocking my pistol.

The man froze in motion as Ward hit the kid one more time, sending him careening off the bar to the floor. When he sat up, he was holding his hand to his mouth and I thought I saw one of his front teeth chipped off.

"I think you folks had better leave while you can," a voice said from the doorway. "All of you." I hadn't noticed the sheriff enter, but the sight of his own drawn gun was enough to know I didn't want to quarrel with the man or his badge.

I stuck my Colt back in my belt and Lotty handed me my bowie. The barkeep moved to the center of the floor and picked up two double eagles. When Ward went through his pockets and said they were his, the man silently pocketed them.

"Call it damage money," he said. My side hurt and when I reached behind the bar and pulled out a couple of bottles of his homemade whiskey, he said, "You ain't gonna drink that, are you?"

"Hell, no," I said. "I'm gonna use it for liniment."

Oddly enough, the bottle on the table had gone unharmed and Ward picked it up on the way out.

I looked down at the young lieutenant, who was biting his knuckles, as if producing pain in some other area of his body would reduce the ache in his broken tooth.

"Told you they was godawful painful," I said and then left.

Chapter Five

I slept underneath my wagon that night, as had been
my practice of late. I thoroughly enjoyed the open sky
at night, and hard as the ground was in spots I still
preferred it to a bed. But it sure can bother you when
you wake up in the middle of the night to the downpour
of rain before a storm even starts. At least in Texas
when we had a thunder boomer, there was lightning and
such to accompany it most times. In the part of the
Ohio Valley I had been traveling through, though, the
rain just sort of snuck up on you and dropped a bucket's
worth whenever you were farthest away from your
slicker. So I had taken to sleeping under my wagon as
long as I was in this area.

That whiskey turned out to be just what I needed. I
remembered mountain men like Lije Harper calling it
Tao's Lightning, 'cause it struck hard and fast, but I
had no intention of drinking the stuff. I had heard of
men going blind from drinking two-hundred-proof con-
coctions like that, and I purely had no desire to do that.

Instead, I found a rag and doused it with the liquid and used it as a liniment for the huge blue spot that was forming on my side where the man had continually jabbed at my ribs. And it didn't work half bad.

I had no second thoughts about the soldiers, for the sheriff had led them to the city limits when we left the saloon, with a warning to stay out of town unless they wanted to get real familiar with the inside of his jail cells. And as determined as they seemed to be to get Ward, I had the notion they had had their fill of us, especially after seeing the way Lotty had been able to use that knife on a man. If they had any sense they would head on back to where they came from and forget whatever it was they needed from Ward. After all, the man had a definite dislike of them, wherever it was he knew them from. And common sense said that you could only butt your head against a brick wall so many times before you busted it wide open.

When I turned in, I lay down on my back, hoping I wouldn't turn during the night and wake to the feel of pain in my side. I had injured the same ribs in a fight a few years back and it had been some time before I could sleep comfortable without having to fear that pain in my sleep. But it wouldn't bother me that night.

I lay there thinking of Ellie, and pretty soon I could see her in my dreams. She was the most beautiful woman I had ever met, with long blonde hair that she had a hard time keeping stuck under the hat she wore outdoors, mainly because I was always teasing her about it and pulling the hat off her head. There were times she would get right mad and stomp off for a bit, but I knew she wouldn't stay that way for long. I reckon that was one of the reasons I had married her, knowing that she could never stay mad at me for long.

But while she was . . . Lordy, but that woman was beautiful! She had soft blue eyes that told me one day after the next that she cared for me more than she ever could for anyone else. We each of us knew back at the start, before San Jacinto and especially afterwards, that we'd never need anyone else, not ever. It was four years now and I still missed her when I was away for any length of time, just like those storybook characters Finn was always talking about. I never did take much to the ways they had of fighting a battle, but one thing I couldn't fault them writers on was the way they put down how a man feels about his woman when she's not there. No, siree.

Of course, Ellie had her own way of getting back at me for my teasing. There was mornings I'd wake up feeling what she called the effects of the "day after the night before" even when I was sleeping. The first thing I'd see when I woke up was her smiling face over me. The first thing I'd feel was her hair cascading down along the sides of my face, and a want for her. And somehow I could always tell by that smile that she was going to taunt me with herself until I couldn't stand it no more. And that night it seemed like she was right there in that dream, like I could touch her and feel her soft lips, like I wasn't missing her at all.

When I woke up, Lotty was kissing me hard, her hair falling down past me to the ground. And it wasn't until I knew I wasn't dreaming, knew it wasn't Ellie I was kissing, that I stopped enjoying that kiss. I pushed her away and she hit her head on the wagon bottom.

"Ouch!"

"What the hell are you trying to do?" I blurted out, then lowered my voice, thinking Ward was somewhere near and would hear me. "Are you trying to get me killed? Where is Ward, anyway?"

She smiled, pointing a thumb at the wagon bottom, indicating Ward must be inside the wagon.

"Are you crazy?" I said, still trying to hold down the tone of my voice, at the same time automatically reaching for my Colt to check the loads. Thirty-five was considered a ripe old age then, figuring the hazards of frontier life, but it was still too young in my mind for dying at the hands of a jealous husband when it ain't your fault to begin with.

"Don't worry," she said, still smiling, "he's drunk as a lord. Besides, I thought you were enjoying that for a minute." Then she leaned forward again to kiss me but I planted a free hand on her chest and pushed her back.

"Get away, woman," I said impatiently. "I've got enough trouble as it is."

She said nothing, working her way out from under the wagon as I turned to do the same out of force of habit and found myself grimacing at the pain shooting through my side.

"You look like you could use some doctoring," she said as I crawled out, my face still looking like I was feeling. "Where do you keep your medical supplies? Or do you have any?" She was talking in her normal tone of voice as though nothing were going to happen. Me, I was feeling the palms of my hands begin to sweat around that Colt.

"Inside the back of the wagon," I all but whispered.

She casually walked to the back of the wagon, fumbled around inside until she found what she was looking for and returned. In her hands she carried the half-empty bottle of whiskey I had used for a liniment along with some other medicinals. It was nearing daybreak and without a word we set about our individual chores, she heating some water for whatever doctoring she thought she could do on me that I hadn't experimented with already, and me throwing a handful of coffee beans into the pot of water and setting it to boil.

I was leaning against the wagon wheel, watching the bright streaks of red and orange appear on the horizon, when she handed me a cup of coffee and set down her medicinals on the water barrel.

"It is kind of pretty, isn't it?" she said matter-of-factly, as though she could read my thoughts.

"Yes, ma'am. Makes a body appreciate the day more, I always thought." I took a sip of my coffee, remembering days when I would have given anything to see the sun.

"Sort of your sign of hope, then?" Before I could answer, she had put her arms around me, stopping when I froze stiff. "I'm only going to check your side, Mr. Callahan," she said, then lifted my shirt to look at my makeshift bandage.

"Yes, ma'am, I reckon you could say that." I paused. "Only one sight I like better and that's the sunset."

"Oh?" She said it with only half an interest, concentrating on the bruise and what she could do to it.

"That's a fact. Way I see it, morning light makes me want to finish out the day just so's I can get to the end of it and see those colors in reverse." And like it or not, that was the truth, for there had been days when I had my doubts about whether or not I'd see the end of my life before the end of that day. Thinking back on it, that was probably what kept me going in the back of my mind, what made me get out of those scrapes.

I didn't say much after that, just stood and finished

my coffee and watching the sun come up, flinching every once in a while when she touched a tender spot.

"One thing about you men," she said when she was through.

"Ma'am?"

She smiled. "You're all so anxious to prove how tough you are when it comes to fighting, but when you need doctoring you've got the same feeling of pain as the rest of us."

I raised an eyebrow, as thought to admit her right. "One of my weaknesses, I reckon."

She turned back to her medicinals then and tossed out the water, setting the pan on the top of the rain barrel. But I wasn't prepared for what I saw when she looked at me again. I wouldn't have put it past her to buy a man's shirt a size too small to do it, or maybe it was just the buttons on the shirt. But she had that longing look on her face and when she breathed in, a button or two that hadn't come undone yet did just that, and part of her . . . self was about to fall out.

"Are you sure there aren't any other weaknesses?" She said it in that way of hers—sultry was how Finn called it. To me it was a wanting voice that had a bit of plea in it, only I wasn't sure it was for me or for what might be.

"No, ma'am," I said, gulping hard, "I reckon that's the only one." Then I found the buttons on her shirt and redid them.

"And just what do you think you're doing?" she asked in a huff.

"Sun ain't up yet, ma'am," I said, continuing to rebutton her shirt. " 'Tain't that warm. Now, you wouldn't want to catch your death, would you?" She stood there, speechless, the anger in her eyes the killing kind of a person who likes to play jokes but can't stand being the butt of them. I took a short step to the fire and poured myself more coffee before I looked back at her with a smile. "Or lose something?"

I do believe she would have given me a piece of her mind, if nothing else, if it hadn't been for Ward making noises inside the wagon and stumbling around until he could make his way out. He had the look of a man who is used to a hangover but dislikes them nonetheless. He seemed grateful for the cup of coffee I handed him, but I thought I saw a vengeful look on Lotty's face from the corner of my eye, too. When I smiled, it seemed to make her that much madder, and she stomped off to do other things.

I stopped by Fanny's on the way out of town. She had agreed to sell me some of her side meat the evening before, but when I reached in my pocket to pay her, she would have none of it.

"I've a soft heart when it comes to the Irish, Nathan," she said with a smile. "But one thing."

"Name it," I said.

"Someday you must bring your lovely wife and child to see me."

I took her tiny hand in mine, squeezed it, and kissed her gently on the forehead. "You bet, Fanny." A tear came to her eye and with all the trouble I had with women, the one thing I couldn't handle was crying. I smiled. "You keep these fellas in line and take care of yourself."

Then I climbed up on the driver's box and let out a few cuss words as my team moved forward. I didn't look back, pretty sure I'd know what I'd see and not wanting to.

I spent the better part of the morning enjoying the fresh air and the wilderness. There are times a man can be alone and feel a kindred spirit with his Maker. All a person had to do was take in the lay of the land. I knew good and well that where I was heading in Texas there was no greenery to compare to what I was traveling through right now.

And part of the good I was feeling was in knowing that I had finally left the Wards behind to fare for themselves. They had been nothing but trouble for me since I had met them, both of them causing a good share of it. So you might say that even if there was trouble along the trail, I at least had my own choice about what I would do to handle it. No outsiders to sway me in one direction or another. Besides, it was the way a man was supposed to handle his life.

I was about to make noon camp when I saw them coming. Like all of them back east, you could hear them before you saw them. I started cussing when I could tell for sure it was them, and I was still cussing when they rode into camp free as you please and dismounted.

It was the Wards.

"I thought I left you back in town."

Ward shrugged, then smiled as though he were playing high stakes poker and had an ace up his sleeve. It was a look I didn't like.

"You did, but I got to thinking." I didn't say anything, instead took a bite of my hardtack and jerked beef, waiting for him to lay out his cards. "You see, Callahan, it occurred to me that you need a guard for this little arsenal you're carrying." When I frowned, he said, "Oh, yes, I know about your shipment of arms. After all, I slept on them last night. And your friend, Colt, likes to advertise quite a bit."

It was then I remembered that the boxes had Sam Colt's trademark and company name on nearly all sides of them. The thing to do would have been to call him out on it, tell him right off that I had no use, nor did I want, to do any more traveling with him or his wife. But there was something in the back of my mind that had been bothering me about ex-Sergeant Joseph Ward, and I found myself asking about it instead of just thinking.

"Were those soldiers really after you for desertion back there?"

"Hell, no!" he said with a smile. When he saw it wouldn't do as an answer to my question, he added, "Look, Callahan, those men got me drunk one night and the next morning told me I'd signed up for another hitch when I hadn't. I was planning on getting out and trying my luck somewhere else." I was still frowning at him when he said, "They do it all the time!"

"Joseph was one of their best sergeants," Lotty said, trying to sound supportive. He might have been a good sergeant, but I had the notion she was saying it more for his benefit than from any firsthand knowledge she might have had about his soldiering.

"So, you just decided to travel west."

"Yup," he said, walking toward his mount.

"With me."

"That's a fact." He reached inside his bed roll, pulled out a bottle of whiskey.

"I don't travel with drunks," I said as he was hoisting the bottle to his lips. He stopped in midmotion and gave me a hard look, as though he couldn't believe I had the audacity to say such a thing. I stood up, looked at him just as hard. "You travel with me, this is my outfit, I give the orders. No booze."

He glanced at Lotty then back at me before he shrugged and smiled. "Fair enough. You've got a deal."

I thought if I could keep him sober he might come in handy.

The woman was a whole different problem.

Chapter Six

Lotty Ward didn't turn out to be a problem at all. In fact, she made the whole long trip a bit more pleasurable by adding something to the cooking. Most women can do a right fine job of making a better than decent meal, if you give them a chance. They were brought up to do all of the chores a woman was supposed to do from dawn to dusk, and somewhere along the way they usually picked up a trick or two from their mothers on how to please a man with a meal. Of course, knowing you didn't have to eat your own cooking day after day usually had something to do with how a meal tasted, too. I don't know what she did to the game that Ward and me provided, but it tasted almighty good.

During the time we were on the trail the both of them seemed to tone down from the way they had acted. Lotty got to being pleasant and conversational, not at all as brazen as the woman I had been dealing with. And Ward even sounded civilized in the way he said and did things. Or maybe he was finding out what life was like when you didn't live it in a bottle, and it was taking to him. Or the other way around. Whatever it was, he hadn't forgotten his military training, for he seemed to follow orders without question and, I thought, with a good deal of common sense. The only questions he had were raised at night over the campfire in the period of evening between supper and sundown that a body usually reserves for easing up on the bit some. He had a real urge to know about the land he was going into and said so one night.

"Well, hoss, most of it ain't nothing like what you're seeing right now," I said, trying to think how best to describe it. "It's a big land that runs in stretches, I reckon you'd say. Nothing like here, where you've got hills and trees and then a stretch of open land afore you. No, sir." I paused, not sure I was saying it right, knowing that Finn was a lot better at speechifying than I would ever be. "I ain't for sure if it's how the Maker meant for it to be, but you can bet on one thing, Ward."

"Oh?"

"Yeah. When you see it, you'll know it was made for a survivor." He frowned and I continued. "There's stretches of flat land that'll make you think you can see into forever—they're that long. And mountain ranges that're so high they put anything else you ever seen, or will see, to shame! I tell you, Ward, there's a lot of beautiful country out there. Thing is, a man ain't careful he might not live to see the all of it, for it's just as dangerous as it is beautiful."

"How's that?"

"Well, I reckon it's kind of like drifting through Indian country. You ever fought Indians?"

"Seminoles," he said, "in the war a couple years back."

"Then you know what I mean. It's the newness of the country that kills a lot of people. They see all this new land and they get so taken by it that they let down their guard and pretty soon they find their scalps at the end of some coup stick. Or they get flooded out or burned out 'cause they never give thought to what spring thaw brings or just how hot it really can get in the summer.

"What you gotta do is learn to live with the land, not change it. They ain't a helluva lot of men ever fought this land and its elements and lived to tell about it."

"Then what are we to do, if this land is as beautiful as you say, Mr. Callahan?" Lotty asked. "Simply ignore what is there?"

"No, ma'am. I was you, I'd take to admiring what you can see and like it from a distance. Don't get too close to it until you get used to it, until you can take care of yourself and what you see and do comes second nature to you. Then you can admire it all you want. Yes, ma'am. But first you've got to learn to survive in it."

Neither of them said much about it afterwards, and the only thing I could figure was that I hadn't said it the right way or they had had their fill of what I had said. The truth was it felt sort of queer, what with them acting like most husband and wives rather than the rowdy couple I'd first met. Either they were reforming or they were after something, and somehow the thought of these two changing their ways overnight didn't strike true at all. But stranger things had happened, even in Finn's storybooks.

It wasn't until we were out of the Ohio Valley and

across the Mississippi that I started giving out names of places I recognized as we made our way deeper into Texas. And, like most pilgrims making their way for the first time into this country, the Wards found that a lot of the names sounded as strange as the places they were named after looked.

"Knew a fella farther south, one time," I said, just to make conversation when I saw the confused look on Lotty's face after hearing what I had called one valley. "Set up a farm, he did. Trouble was his livestock kept getting spooked and he was losing what few chickens he had right fast."

"You're quite a storyteller, Mr. Callahan," Lotty said, a suspicious grin coming to her face. "This wouldn't be another of those wild stories that stretch the imagination that you tell at night, would it?"

"No, ma'am," I said, straight-faced. "This 'un's the for-sure truth." Not that I hadn't stretched the blanket some to pass the time at night, for I'd admit to doing that. I could tell some real hair-raisers when it come down to it. And maybe that was the trouble with them stories: sometimes they was hard telling where the imagination left off and the actual event took place.

"This fella come on a rattlesnake one morning as it was about to do in one of his hens." I smiled, remembering the man who had originally told the story.

"I suppose that menial bit of information has a lot to do with your story?"

"Well, I reckon you could say so, ma'am. You see, old Gar, he'd taken a real likin' to having fresh eggs on a regular basis, and when he killed that rattler and found its kind was the cause of all his trouble . . . well, ma'am, he took out after every one he could find. Fact is, he spent the all of one summer hunting 'em out in a canyon near his spread. Said he killed seventy of 'em that summer.'' I paused as Lotty's face took on a sickly look and she got a little green around the gills.

"That many?!" she said, in awe of the number. "My God, I hope he got rid of them! I don't think I could stand the sight of one!" She visibly shivered as she spoke now.

"Now, Lotty, you've got to remember that in this land you make do as best you can with what you have, and that's just what Gar did afore he got rid of them sidewinders.''

"You mean he—"

"Yes, ma'am, milked 'em, skinned 'em and ate 'em." Lotty was looking greener at the gills and turning a shade whiter the more I talked, and I found myself enjoying what I was saying. You might say it was a way of getting back at her for the torment she had put me through earlier. "Gar says they's a right tasty diversion from salt pork and red meat. Fricasee's the way he fixes 'em.

"But you know what the best thing about them rattlers was?" She gave me a look that said she could not believe there could be any more horrifying aspect of the story to be told. "He made hatbands and belts out'n 'em, yes, ma'am.''

I lifted my shirt to reveal a snakeskin belt at my waist.

"See," I said, grinning.

Her face went ghost-white and suddenly she was digging her heels into her mount, heading for a clump of trees in the distance. Through it all, Ward had seemed to enjoy watching her squirm as I told my story. I saw him grin as he pulled up alongside the wagon.

"Callahan, you may be one of the few men who ever found a way of putting her in her place." Then, studying my belt, he said, "That really snakeskin?"

I nodded, grinning my own self, for there was the same feeling of satisfaction as Ward had said. And it may have been the only thing the two of us ever had in common.

I watched her in the distance, knowing that whatever she had had for breakfast was being upchucked then and there. There must have been a crooked smile come to my face as I watched her, for I then saw Ward looking at me, cocking a curious eye at me, the way a body does when they want to know what's behind your smile but don't want to say so.

When I looked at him, I said, "Just wait till I tell her what old Gar did with the rattles."

There is something about being in your own land that makes you feel more comfortable, and that was just how I felt about Texas. Or maybe it was being back among my own family that added to the feeling. Don't ever let a man tell you that belonging don't mean something to him. Pa had said it in a roundabout way some years back and I'd not forgotten it. But then, with Ellie and little James to be around me, I didn't often have to be reminded.

James had been born in the spring of '37, a year most would never forget, because of the depression back east. Me, I'll remember it for Ellie giving birth to our first son. And there was no denying that it tickled Finn to have himself be called an uncle at the age of fifteen. But that was three years ago and things had changed since then. James was growing fast, a big lad for his age, a fact that gave hint to him probably turning out to

be my size or better, and I'm no small man. And Finn
had changed some, too.

When he first came west, it was following me to
prove he could be as much a man as I was. There was
sixteen years' difference between the two of us, not to
mention a whole lot of experience, and I honest to God
didn't think he had it in him. But Finn, he was as feisty
as a wild bronc and made up in guts for what he lacked
in stature. He had proved himself at the Battle of San
Jacinto in '36 and now it was some four years later and
he was his own man for sure. He had gone from a
gangly fourteen-year-old kid to a man of eighteen, a
man to be reckoned with at that. And aside from Finn
being the educated one in the family, there was only
one other difference between us and that was size. Me,
I was over six foot and close to two hundred pounds as
near as I could figure, and thick in the arms, chest, and
legs, although I don't say that to brag. Finn, now, he
had shot up to six foot, but the lad was wiry, lean, if
you like to call it that, and I often wondered if he could
hold his own in a fandango. He went ahead and rid me
of any thoughts to the contrary one time when we got
into a fight in a cantina in San Antone. It was the two
of us against some rowdies, six or so as I recall, and I
figured that even back to back I was going to wind up
doing most of the fighting my own self. And that's
when Finn surprised me, for the boy made up for in
speed and a quick punch what he lacked in bulk. It was
then I realized that if anyone knew the truth of a man
having to make do with what he had, it was Finn. And
he did a right good job of it. And had been ever since.

After Texas won its independence, it became a popular place to settle down and try your hand at a new life,
if you'd a mind to. Cooper Hansen, an old storyteller I

had grown up with, had often spoken of how Jim Harrod and Daniel Boone had opened up the Kentucky wilderness and how it was only after they had done this that settlers came to make a life for themselves. And after San Jacinto I got to wondering if the same wasn't happening to Texas. I had heard how Boone had wound up leaving Boonesboro because his nearest neighbor was some seventeen miles from him and he figured civilization was closing in on him, and it struck me that some of the original Austin colony might wind up doing the same in Texas.

San Antonio had become an easygoing town, a mixture of Mexican and whites who, for the most part, managed to live together in peace; they shared one common bond, that being the fear of the Comanche as he fought for his own land. But most folks had come to accept the threat of an occasional Indian raid as being as much a part of the hazards of the frontier as the droughts and floods. Not that you ever got used to them; you simply accepted them for what they were.

Ben McCulloch and Jack Hays were at Ranger headquarters when I pulled the Conestoga up in front of the building. McCulloch had gotten to Texas just in time to command the "Twin Sisters," the two cannons— and only artillery—we had at San Jacinto in '36, but he'd drifted into surveying and politics afterwards. He had been born and raised in Tennessee, laying claim to being a personal friend of Davy Crockett before Crockett came to Texas and died at the Alamo with Bowie. But he had kept in touch with the rest of us who had taken to the Rangers—Hays, Sam Walker, and my own self—and was a man who could be counted on when the need arose. And the way Ben and Jack were palavering when I pulled up, I had a notion that maybe that

time had come, for they looked almighty serious about
their discussion. So much, in fact, that neither one
noticed me, the Wards, or the wagon when we came to
a halt.

"Which one of you is worrying the other with his
war stories?" I asked and saw a grin spread across the
faces of both men as they looked up.

"Well, I'll be," Hays said, as though astonished to
see me at all. "Why, I figured the earth done swallowed you up." Then, with a grin, he nudged McCulloch.
"See, Ben, I told you Nathan wouldn't sell out those
guns just to make a profit."

"Almost had 'em took from me," I said, climbing
down from the wagon. "If you ain't afraid of lifting
something heavier than your saddle, let's get these
inside and I'll tell you about it."

I introduced the Wards and we unloaded the rifles
and pistols. Jack poured coffee all around and I knew
from the look on Lotty's face that it had either been
boiling for some time or had been made to float a
horseshoe, it was that bitter. But no ranger ever complained about it, for many's the time a cup of coffee
was all his stomach got, along with a chew of beef
jerky, between can-see and can't-see.

I gave a brief accounting of the three highwaymen
and Ward's stepping in like he did. It probably sounded
like that was when I had first met them, for I omitted
the encounter in New York as well as the one with the
army on the way back to Texas. Anything else that had
happened was nobody's business. Besides, I'd just as
soon forget it.

"How're Ellie and James?" I asked, changing the
subject.

"Just fine, Nate, just fine," Jack said. "She got an

invite to socialize with Martha and some of the other ladies over at Linnville earlier in the week, so Finn took her and the boy over for a few days. Ought to be back tomorrow, I reckon.''

"Good." I took a sip of the coffee, knowing Finn would take care of my wife and son. In fact, I had not felt worried at all when I had left some five montns ago to go to New York. Some may have thought of Finn as a working hand on the ranch we were building, but Ellie treated him just like family and always would. One thing us Callahans are strong on is family.

"Now, tell me what you two looked so all-fired serious about when I drove up. I didn't see much sign of hostiles on the way in. Did Karnes and his boys bring off that talk they were gonna have with the Comanch'?''

Ever since the land had opened up and more settlers had come in, the Comanches in the area had become more active with their occasional raids. Not that they could be blamed in a sense, for it was their land long before the white man a..d Spaniard had come. But the sad truth was that the land was no longer theirs, for it was being taken from them, bit by bit, day by day, year by year. When the early conquistadors had come, the Indians had been introduced to the horse, which .may well have been the only decent thing done for them. The Spanish had forced them to move north, where they were not annihilated completely, and it must have seemed that each generation found itself fighting for survival against more of the invaders of their land. The bow and arrow were no match for the flintlock musket and percussion weapons just recently developed, but the Indian made up for it with his uncommon mastery as a horseman and guerrilla warrior. The fact was that the

Comanche in this area seemed particularly determined to drive out the white man or any other people who tried to inhabit his land. But Henry Karnes and some of the others had thought it possible to meet with the chieftains of the various tribes and work out some kind of peace agreement. That was just before I left.

"Those Comanche were what we were discussing when you came in, Nathan," Ben said a bit reluctantly. "And the Council House Fight . . . well, I've a feeling we may never be at peace with the Comanches after what happened there." Then, between the two of them, they told what had happened as Ward, Lotty, and I listened.

The idea of obtaining some kind of peace was still a good one when arrangements had been made to meet with some of the Comanche at the San Antonio courthouse for a peace council. Out of a total of sixty-five Indians, women and children included, some twelve warriors had shown up with their chief. With them they brought a fifteen-year-old girl who had been a captive of theirs for two years. The Indians had quickly been surrounded by three companies of infantry and told to turn over all of their hostages before they would be set loose their own selves. A shooting fight had followed, with seven whites and thirty-some Indians, nearly half of their force, being killed, and a good many of the Indian women and children being taken prisoner. A squaw had been sent to inform the other Comanches of the terms being set, but only two or three other captives were ever returned.

"Word went out shortly after that that the southern Comanche were so angered at what we did, they put to death some thirteen of their white prisoners," Hays said. "No one's been able to confirm it one way or another yet, so your guess is as good as mine, Nate."

"Sounds kind of stupid to me," Ward said, "asking somebody in for a council talk and then declaring war on them because they were dumb enough to take you at your word."

"I'd have to agree," McCulloch said. "It's not exactly the most intelligent thing ever done."

"Is that why I didn't see much of them on the way in?" I asked.

"Well, Nate, that's the strange part," Hays said. "In fact, that's what we were talking about when you rode in."

"That's right," Ben said. "You see, there hasn't been any hostile activity since the Council House Fight at all. And there are some who say the Comanche has learned his lesson, that he'll stay away from us and our settlements now. Jack and I were saying they're up to something."

"Yeah, it's too damn quiet to suit me."

"You're probably right," Ward said, speaking up again. "No Indian is gonna quit just because you do in a couple of dozen of their own. Hell, you'd have to do in half their nation before they'd cut and run. I know it sure seemed like that when we fought the Seminoles in Florida."

"I'll go along with that," I said, and found myself wondering just how safe Ellie and James were, even with Finn being there to protect them. It was sounding more and more like they weren't.

Ben McCulloch had to leave then, and to keep from thinking too much on what might be happening, I told Jack Hays I'd give whatever Rangers were handy a lesson in how to use these new weapons if he could round them up that afternoon. He agreed and I set about unpacking them, Ward giving me a hand. The ex-sergeant had heard everything Hays and McCulloch had said, including the part about Finn taking Ellie and James on down to Linnville. If he knew what was running through my mind he didn't say so, and I gave him credit for knowing that there are some things a man won't discuss unless it's with a friend, and I didn't exactly figure me and Ward for being on anything close to those terms. But it didn't stop Lotty from speaking her mind when she brought us some coffee after a bit.

"You love her very much, don't you?" she said while I took a sip of the hot liquid.

"Yes," I said, my shortness of temper showing. "Why do you ask?"

"There are some things a woman can tell," she said, shooting Ward a quick glance. At first I wasn't sure if she was laying out bait for another foofaraw between me and her husband again or what, but when she looked at me next, it was with a knowing look and a voice to match.

"When your friend mentioned where she had gone, you balled your fist up as though you were ready to fight," she said as though she were stating a simple fact. "And when something happens that you have no control over, something that bothers you—and this bothers you, Mr. Callahan—you find something to do until you think you have an answer to your problems." I sat there, dumbfounded, for it was almost as if she were reading my mind. She smiled. "There are things a woman knows." She paused a moment, a more serious look taking over her face. "She knows. And if I were a gambler, I'd bet money that she's told you, too."

"If you were a gambler, you'd win," I said in an

even tone. "But that still wouldn't make it any of your business."

I would have cussed her out then and there, husband or no husband, but a group of buckskin-clad men came in and I knew Hays had succeeded in finding a good share of the men who were not out chasing someone.

We moved everything out back and I took my time telling them how much of an improvement the new Model Number 5 was over the old Paterson. Only a handful had ever seen or operated the revolving rifle before and most expressed a good deal of faith in both the hand gun and the rifle. It would give them an edge when it came to fighting groups of Indians that outnumbered them, and when a man has an edge he can be a goodly deal more confident of what he's about. I was about to show them the revolving shotgun and how it worked but never got the chance. My life was getting to be full of interruptions and it wasn't making me feel any better.

He came stumbling through the back door, wearing enough blood to look like he had been fighting a grizzly for a wintering spot.

"Comanch'!" he said, looking crazed and scared at the same time. "They raided it! Lavaca, they did!" Then he fell to the ground, unconscious.

Lavaca was halfway between us and Linnville, maybe thirty miles off, but it didn't seem to matter where it was, for all I could think of was what direction the raid had come from. A couple of the Rangers got some water and brought the man to. As it turned out, a good share of the blood on him had come from others who'd been caught in the fight, his own wounds being in the fleshy part of his shoulder and leg.

"How many were there?" Hays asked when he came to.

"Hundreds of them!" the man exclaimed. "Maybe thousands!" He was talking like it was his last breath, but I had a notion he was more scared than anything else. "They was only three of us left when we got to the horses. And now there's only . . ."

"You rest easy, friend," Hays said, then told one of the others to fetch a doctor. "We'll talk later."

Linnville was near the coast, which made Lavaca closer, and I only had one thing going through my mind. I was wanting to know which direction those Comanche had come from. Had they already been to Linnville? Or were they working their way southward, away from us? The fella on the ground wasn't making a whole lot of sense, but I had to know what had happened to Ellie, whether she was alive or not. I was picking up a couple of the Model 5s when I heard Jack Hays behind me.

"What do you think you're doing?"

"You said Ellie, James, and Finn were at Linnville," I said, grabbing a revolving rifle. "I gotta know, Jack. One way or another, I gotta know."

"Won't do you any good, Nate." When I frowned, he added, "It'll be dark in an hour or two." He was right about that, and I'd not yet seen a horse that could track in the dark. Or a man, either. "Why not wait until morning? We'll get an early start and pick up their trail then. Besides, Nate, if something did happen . . . well, there isn't much you or anyone else can do about it right now."

"He's right, Callahan," Ward said, picking up one of the rifles and testing its heft. "And you know it." Then a mischievous smile came to his face. "Almost two, three years since I fought Injuns. Be a change for me.''

"Yancy," Jack Hays said to one of the men, "you take a couple of the boys and spread the word. We're leaving at dawn tomorrow. I want to get at least fifty men to go with us." The man turned to leave and Hays spoke again. "And Yancy."

"Yeah, boss."

"If they complain about not having the weapons for it," he said, looking down at the new Colt guns, "you tell 'em we'll furnish 'em."

Chapter Seven

People that are new to this country tend to get rattled easier than those that have been here awhile. Not that it ought to be held against them or anything, but I'll tell you, they sure can see things that ain't there a whole lot quicker than a body that's used to the country will. And that's how it was with that fella that came staggering into Ranger headquarters that day.

We were up and gone by sunup the next day, which was probably about the time Lotty went to bed. Most of the men were there an hour before we figured to leave and it was purely a surprise to find that Lotty had been up the better part of the night fixing food for those that made it in on time. She had enough coffee for a small army, and from the number of men I saw ride in, that was about what I figured we had. There were upwards of fifty just like Jack Hays wanted, and with the exception of a couple of latecomers, Lotty fed the whole bunch of them.

Hays and the rest took along their normal supply of

gunpowder and caps and balls for the new weapons, probably figuring to chase those Comanches a ways out of the territory and come on back until next time. Me, I found a mochila bag and added in some extra shot and powder and tied it good and tight to the back of my saddle, laying my slicker right atop it. I got some strange looks from some of the men, but it didn't make a damn to me then. They might have been going out to play pot shot with the Comanch' for a couple of days, but I was looking for my wife and son and I wasn't stopping until I found them. And if they wasn't no more . . . well, there was going to be some awful dead Indians put to rest before they buried me. That was for damn sure!

Like I said, that pilgrim that came in kind of stretched the blanket some on his numbers when he sighted the Comanches that had burned out his village. It was near noon of the first day that we came across Ben McCulloch and a couple dozen men. They had gotten word of the raiding early yesterday afternoon and had taken off after the Comanches. From what Ben was saying, it wasn't nothing close to a thousand warriors that had burned that village.

"We circled the town and figure close to thirty of them, but no more," Ben said.

It made me feel a bit easier, knowing that. Linnville was a sight bigger than Lavaca and if every man in town had at least one weapon, it stood to reason they shouldn't have that much trouble with thirty or so renegades if they stuck together. I knew that Finn would do everything he could to fight them off, with Ellie probably standing right beside him doing the reloading. She was that kind of woman.

We joined forces and moved into the Big Hill country,

an area on the divide between the tributaries of the
Guadalupe and the Lavaca rivers. It was there we joined
forces again, this time with John Tumlinson, a man
known in his own right as one hell of a good Indian
fighter, and his group of men. He had been out looking
for Comanches, too, so with the all of us put together,
we had some hundred and a quarter men. Not a bad-
size group when you considered the fact that even if the
Indians who had raided Lavaca were only thirty in
number, it wouldn't take the Comanche nation long at
all to summon up a good thousand warriors to get real
serious about doing away with the white man.

We rode south to Victoria, but the Comanche had
already been there when we arrived at sunset. Some of
us circled the town before the sun was totally down and
between us came up with some fifteen hundred, maybe
two thousand, tracks, indicating the renegades were
either out in force or had stolen every horse they could
lay their hands on since the killing began. One thing
was for sure. There was a sight more than twenty or
thirty of them now.

Except for a small group of men left behind to bury
the thirteen who had been killed at Victoria, we were
on the trail at daybreak. I had taken to scouting the
forward of us and it was noon when I first saw the
smoke of the burning buildings of Linnville. I waved
the others on and gave the grulla full rein, riding hell-
for-leather for the town.

You can tell when something's been burned out, for
it gives off a heat that is equal only to the sun on its
hottest day. And I could feel that heat riding toward
that town. When the wind shifted slightly, I caught a
whiff of the burned smell of wood and 'dobe mixed
together . . . and flesh. It made me ride that much

harder. I had the Colt in my hand when I rode into town, but it was of little use.

I was expecting Indians, but the movement I had seen getting closer turned out to be what I thought were some of the townspeople, moving about here and there. Looking about I could see that if it was made of wood it no longer existed in this world. The grulla was getting skittish at the stench of burned flesh and the presence of heat and I could not blame it. I pulled up in front of one man who seemed not to notice me as the rest of the rangers entered town.

"What happened here, mister?"

"Kind of late, aren't you?" was all he said, his face a total blank. It was pretty clear he was a bit out of his head, but I had other things on my mind and, after dismounting, I grabbed him by the shoulders, trying to shake some sense into him.

"Look, mister, I got a wife, son, and brother that was in this town just recently and I gotta know where they are."

"Easy, Nate," Jack Hays said, dismounting. "If Ellie and the others were here, we'll get to it." Then he handed the man his canteen and slowly coaxed the pieces of what had happened out of him. I stood there listening impatiently, my fists balled up with that help-less feeling about me.

It was the same bunch of Comanches we had been trailing, for the man said they had come from the Victoria end of town, meaning the north side. For some reason or another, the number of residents now in town had been some two miles out of town when they saw the Indians coming. Except they didn't figure them for Indians, more like a Mexican caravan of traders. The Comanches had approached the town at full speed, riding in a half-moon formation so as to surround the place as quick as they could. Maybe it was their numbers that scared them off, but the rest of the people in town fled as fast as they could. Somehow I just didn't believe the story that there wasn't a single weapon to be found in town to fight with! That was too far-fetched to be believable.

The raiders had stayed the whole day, taking their own time and burning each house down individually, ransacking it before they did. They had also taken their knives and lances to whatever beeves they could find, which accounted for the stench I had smelled on the way in, for they had burned the remains in a corral at the edge of town. While all this was taking place, those who had escaped were within sight of the town, forced to witness the destruction of their own property, knowing they could not do a damn thing about it.

But not everyone had survived. There had been five men killed in the raid and, if what this man said was correct, the Comanches had made off with a couple other women and a child. When I heard that I wasn't sure if I should feel some kind of relief knowing that they were still alive, or pity for them, for I knew all too well how they would wind up as hostages of the Comanche. That left only Finn's whereabouts unknown, and I decided I had had enough and must have looked as mean as I was feeling.

"Mister, I got the same question for you I had a couple of minutes back. I come looking for my wife, son, and brother. Now, as much as you've told about this raid and all, you must know something about them." He still looked dazed and out of sorts, but at least Jack Hays and the others had the good sense not to butt in this time. Like I said, the Callahans are strong on family.

"Ellie is her name," I continued. "She's tall for a woman, young and blonde. The boy's three years, got the same blond hair. Finn is my brother, tall, sort of lanky, a friendly sort."

"Oh," he said, and I thought I saw a glimmer of memory in his eyes. "The crazy one, you mean."

"Crazy one? What are you talking about?"

"Yup," he said, chuckling as though the whole memory were amusing. "Only one here that had a sidearm; fought those Indians from house to house, he did. Had the woman and child you describe with him." He paused a moment, reflecting. "Until they got him. Took the woman and boy."

"Got him?" My blood was boiling now and I knew that if I didn't get the rest of the story right quick I was going to grab ahold of this fella and shake it out of him one way or another.

"You'll find him, yonder, in those buildings," he said, pointing to one of the two 'dobe structures that had not burned.

Right then I didn't care what Hays, McCulloch, or the rest did. I only had one thing on my mind, and that was finding Finn and, more importantly, finding out if he was dead or alive. I swung up into the saddle and spurred the grulla to the far side of town.

Inside the 'dobe it was dark and I had to wait for my eyes to adjust before I could see anything. It was probably the coolest place in town and of that I was glad, for it was August now and no matter what they said about the Fourth of July heat in Texas, August could come up with some fearsome heat of its own.

"Señor?" a woman said, startling me, and I found

myself reaching for the Colt, stopping as I began to
make things out. The woman was a small, portly Mexican and the 'dobe had been turned into a makeshift
hospital of sorts, with people scattered all over the
place and laid out on the floor.

"I'm looking for my brother, Finn Callahan," I said.
"I—"

"Nate?"

The voice came from the left and halfway down the
aisle, but I knew it was Finn's. I wanted to slap him on
the back and tell him how glad I was to see him, but
walking down that aisle I could see that was not to be.
He had large patches of bandages on his shoulder and
his side and two different ones on his leg. So instead I
looked down at him dead serious.

"You're gonna have to stop this, boy. You're making me look bad." When he frowned in puzzlement, I
smiled. "Every time I need you, you go out and get
yourself shot all to hell and gone."

I knelt down beside him and his smile broadened and
he knew I was funning him like I had always done. I
was sixteen years older and prodded him a good deal about
it, but Finn was good-natured to begin with and I knew
he would never be living in my shadow or trying to
measure up to me. He was his own man and we both
knew it, so he took my funning in stride. But of a
sudden I didn't feel all that much like joshing. He was
looking a bit peaked and those four bandages had me
worried.

"How you doing, Finn?"

He smiled, making light of my question.

"It took a skinning knife and three arrows to get me
off their backs," he said.

There was a silence then, the kind where you've got

to know something and you're scared to hell of saying anything and wishing the other person would speak up first. Me, I knew Finn had done everything he could to protect Ellie and James, but there was still the matter of finding them . . . if they were still alive. And Finn was the only chance I had then of knowing what had happened to them. But he was my brother, too, and as desperate as I was to find Ellie and James, I couldn't bring myself to ask him how he had failed. A man just didn't do that to his brother. It simply was not done.

"We fought 'em house to house, Nate," Finn finally said. "I did everything I could, but they just kept on burning 'em, kept on torching the houses. And I swear I was the only one did any fighting, Nate, 'cause they sure wasn't anyone else doing any shooting. I swear!"

"I know. You probably were the only one did any fighting back. Fella saw me coming in called you the crazy one. I reckon 'cause of what you did."

"Too peace-loving to carry weapons, are they?"

"Too peace-loving or too scared," I said flat out. "Take your pick. Sometimes one's an excuse for the other." Finn was more likely to talk his way out of a fight than me and we both knew it. I had never had any use for trying to palaver or running from a fight when I knew full well there was always room for one more devil's son down under. Me, I figured I'd wind up doing some kind of gate guard at the rear entrance when my time came anyway, so it most often didn't make a difference. Besides, Pa always said the only good thing about going to hell was you meet a lot of friends. And the way I was feeling now, I figured I could charge hell with a bucket of water, put out the fire, and skate on the ice, I was that mad.

"They took their time plundering the stores 'fore

they set 'em to fire,'' Finn said. '' 'Cause I saw some of them putting on white man's shirts, pants, and such when they could.

"You'da been proud of Ellie, Nate. She was with me all the way, just like at San Jacinto, loading while you were firing and then some.

"We worked our way to this place," he said, trying to make out the insides of the building, somehow not sure it was this structure. "Ellie had just handed me the Paterson and I was looking out the window for a target when I heard her scream and caught two of them coming through the side entrance. I dusted both and one from the back stuck an arrow in my leg. I emptied the Colt into a couple more and by that time they had taken up Ellie and James and I had me that skinning knife stuck in my shoulder.

"I don't know if it was the sight of that bowie knife I pulled out or them seeing me yank that skinning knife out'n my shoulder that made 'em leery of me, but I was backed into a wall by then and we sort of called it a Mexican standoff." He stopped short then, looked out the window before glancing back at me. "I'm sorry, Nate. I know I didn't—"

"You done fine, Finn. I've known a lot more men who'd have give up or died outright if they was faced with what you was. You just rest up and get better."

"But what about Ellie and James?" His tone was worrisome.

"That's where I'm heading next. Pick up their trail outside of town and I'll follow 'em to hell or anyplace else they call their stomping grounds, as long as it takes to find Ellie and the boy."

"You mean us, don't you?"

The voice came from behind me and when I turned I

saw the darkened frames of Hays and Ward standing in the doorway.

"The Rangers have got just as much interest in those renegades as you do, Nate," Hays said. He was speaking in his official capacity as a captain of Rangers now, more than he was a friend.

"That's right," Ward said, smiling. "Besides, you don't want to go off and kill that whole thousand Injuns by your lonesome now, do you, Callahan? Just 'cause you got a grudge don't mean you can't leave some for those of us who enjoy the sport."

He was back to being his own self again, Ward was. Even in the darkness of that 'dobe I could see it in his smile and the gleam in his eye. The man was thirsting for blood and not caring what the reason for it was, as long as it was a fight that was brewing. He was also back to running his mouth and I was none too fond of that, either. If he didn't see the anger on my face, I made damn sure he heard it in my voice when I crossed the grounds to him.

"Pa always said there was one sure way of keeping a bee out of your mouth, Ward," I said through grit teeth. Then, before he could say anything, I added, "Keep your mouth shut. I liked you better when you kept your thoughts to yourself." Turning to Finn, I said, "I'll check with you before I leave, brother."

Then I left.

Chapter Eight

We finished out the day in Linnville, giving folks a hand at putting things back in order so they could at least get on with living. A detail was sent out to help them bury the dead and clear away some of the debris, but I had other plans. I was all for helping out your neighbor and all, and would be the first to admit they were in need of it. But me, well, I reckon I had it stuck in my mind that right then I'd rather have a family to be able to help out than neighbors. It was selfish to be sure, but what was a man to do?

I circled the town and sure enough, they had headed west, those Comanch'. Not that they had much choice, for we weren't all that far from the gulf. We had come from the north and the Mexicans had no love for the Comanches, so west was the logical direction to head. Tracking like I was, I remembered what Jack Hays had told us before I left. As near as they could figure, the Comanches had so far either killed or captured close to thirty-some people on this rampage of the last week or so. Jack was thinking maybe the damage they had done so far had been enough revenge for what had happened at Council House, that they might be heading back to their own grounds. And the more I tracked, the more I came to agree with him.

Finn said he had seen them plundering the stores before they burned them, so what Jack said made sense. For the more I tracked the more I was seeing prints that were heavy-laden with more than just a man's weight. It was looking more and more like these raiders had struck their El Dorado and were tying into everything that wasn't nailed down. Seeing that got rid of some of the mad I was feeling, for I knew that greed was going to be the downfall of some of those Indians when we got caught up with them. They weren't traveling light like the warriors of a raiding party anymore. Now they had hostages and horses and supplies, and that meant they had to take time and men to care for them. And what they lost in time we would pick up, even staying the night over in Linnville.

I took Finn his food that night and told him what I had found. He was looking better and was doing mighty good at putting his food away. I had never paid much attention to it until he had come out to the plains with us, but that boy could put away some food and never gain a pound. So I reckon seeing him eat like that made me feel better about him pulling through. I told him I was going to see about getting some of the locals to care for him until he was better, but he already had his own plans.

"That Mexican lady that's been tending me says she'll put me up till I get back on my feet. I figure a couple of days and I'll be able to ride."

"Well, when you do, make sure you head right on back to the spread."

"But what about Ellie and James and the Indians?"

"Don't you worry 'bout Ellie and the boy," I said, standing up. "There ain't no way in hell I ain't coming back without them . . . *alive*." I could tell by the look on his face that Finn wanted to be there in the worst way when I did catch up with those Comanches, and I didn't blame him one bit. We both also knew that him coming along, or trying to catch up with us when he was able to, was about as useful as putting buffalo chips in one of them fancy back-east salads. I wasn't any good with words, not like Finn, and I was pondering just walking away, no matter how he felt, when I smiled and looked down at him. "Look at it this way, kid. Ellie gets back home and finds out that place ain't been tended to, she's liable to give both of us hail Columbia." He gave off a weak smile, nodded his head, but still there was that awkward feeling in the air. He was my brother and he wouldn't expect nothing but the truth and I wouldn't ever give him anything less. So when I looked at him, I tried to sound as determined and hopeful as a body could. "I'm gonna get 'em back, Finn. Don't you worry none 'bout 'em. I'm gonna get 'em back."

"Sure you will, Nate." I was hoping he felt like he looked then, for it surely would ease my notions about him. I looked back at him when I got to the door and somewhere inside I had the idea that just maybe I had said something right in my life.

A pitch-black cup of coffee, a hardtack biscuit and a piece of beef jerky was all we had to hold us before leaving the next morning, but we all knew there would be few of us thinking of food before sunset. There was one thing about working on the frontier, and that was that it left a man little time to think of much else than what he was working at. I reckon that morning the lot of us had catching up with those Comanches on our minds more than anything else. Texas was a big land, but a man got around and odds were that he could find a friend or a friend of a friend in any one of the villages that had been burned out so far. And as hard as times could be, I reckon we all considered each other family of sorts, because when trouble started, especially Indian trouble, the word spread and people just come arunning.

There was proof of that not long after we left camp, as we encountered a courier riding hell-for-leather. It seemed that the president of Texas, Mirabeau Lamar, had gotten wind of what was taking place and authorized a small army of volunteers to be formed until this mess was cleaned up. Turned out there were all sorts of old Indian fighters gathering up forces of their own and just itching to get ahold of some Comanch' afore we could do them all in.

The first day wasn't too bad, for we tracked steady and never came in sight of any of the renegades, although the war party did take a decided turn, heading north by west just past Victoria.

The second and third days were tougher, for we were blinded and stifled, man and horse alike, by the wind and the blowing ashes across the prairie, It was enough to make a body believe that half of Texas had been burned to the ground and was blowing away.

It was the fourth day that we stood down at Plum Creek at day's end. We had come a good ways, some thirty or so miles from Austin, I figured, and there were near two hundred of us now, and if you don't know we were wanting a fight, well, hoss, you needn't have asked. There was a general and some of the militia that had been formed for this fight that arrived, but we voted on a fella named Matt Caldwell to lead the bunch. Ask a man on the plains and he'd tell you that he'd take orders from an Indian fighter any day over someone who called himself a general or something, unless, of course, the general's name was Sam Houston. That was a whole different matter, for Houston had lived with as well as fought Indians in his lifetime, and not a whole lot of men could say that. The plan we drew up was to wait for the Comanches right there at Plum Creek, and you can believe there was a lot of firearms cleaned, reloaded, and checked that night.

Not long before daybreak one of the sentinels came into camp and said they had spotted the Comanches some three miles away. In no time the word had spread and the camp was alive with movement as men readied their mounts as quiet as is possible with that much gear. We spread ourselves out along Plum Creek, concealed by the brush as the Comanche moved diagonally across the prairie that stretched out to our west. When they spotted us they at once formed for battle, and that, my friend, was a sight to see.

Now, one thing you had to give the Comanche credit for and that was he was long on guts. Finn would have called it crazy, but you learned real quick-like in this land that the red man had a hell of a lot more respect for your courage than he ever would for any kind of gold or valuables you might carry. Being able to touch your enemy with a coup stick and come away from it with your own self intact was some kind of brave to those Indians, and for a man to be ready enough to die for an act like that, well, you had to show him at least a grudging respect, no matter how much you might hate him. And fixing to see how much respect they could get was what they were doing right now.

Their order of battle was to line up in one straight line, facing their enemy with I don't know how many deep, and charge like any cavalry you've ever seen straight at you. Only they weren't bluffing. Most of us who had fought them before knew they had only one thing in mind, and that was to strike our line as hard as they could, no matter how many men they might lose, so long as one of them could get to us with those lances they carried. And Lord help the man who got caught on the business end of one of those lances! It was looking like they had us outnumbered at least two or three to one and maybe a smart man who was interested more in his hide than revenge would have cut and run right then. But not the Rangers, and sure not the rest of the men who had lost friends and relatives to the raids. One thing that gave the Rangers confidence was knowing that although that tactic might work well against another tribe using bows and arrows or the Mexicans and their smooth-bore muskets, we had the Colt's repeating rifles and six-guns and that gave a man an edge. Giving us even more of an edge was knowing that most of these Comanch' had not experienced the kind of firepower we could put out.

Watching them now I had the idea I had seen it all before and of a sudden found myself remembering the same type of confrontation at the Battle of San Jacinto that cool April morning. It was an eerie effect, but there they were. Some of the Indians were prancing around with their mounts as if they were showing off the calicos and ribbons that adorned their mounts. It ired me, it purely did. Out of the corner of my eye I thought

I saw some of the men moving a cavvy of horses forward, but my attention was short-lived, for out come one of the chiefs and I swear he could have been Santa Anna all over again!

I remembered how Santa Anna had ridden forward to within shooting range of the Texicans at San Jacinto, sort of flaunting himself before us and his troops when he had arrived. And that seemed to be what this Indian chief, oversized headdress and all, was doing, too. Me, I was itching to get on with it, and I never will understand how I come to do what I did next.

I dismounted and pulled out my Model 5 as I walked out past some brush into the open.

"What the hell do you think you're doing?" someone asked from behind. I never did find out who it was, for I was concentrating on the fella on his horse.

"I didn't come here for no riding show," was all I said as I raised and cocked the Colt. I gave him a lead and aimed high and squeezed that trigger nice and slow. In all that silence there was a large boom as my gun went off and when the breeze blew away the gunpowder a few seconds later, I saw that chief sort of jerk on his horse and fall off, all in one motion. And all at fifty yards!

"Now, general, is your time to charge them!" Caldwell yelled out. "They are whipped!"

While I was remounting, they gave an order and all hell broke loose. All at once those Indians found themselves being charged by a whole bunch of mad Texicans while their herd of horses was beginning to stampede. Pretty soon, in all the confusion, they were stampeded too. All that firepower must have scared them off, for we killed upwards of a hundred in the whole fight, word coming down afterwards that bodies were found tangled up in the brush, in the muddied creek, and even a piece up the San Antonio road.

But I was more interested in those who had survived, and as soon as the shooting stopped I was going through the crowd, searching for the hostages who had still been alive. Of those I found, one of the women had been killed, by who I had no idea. Two more were slightly wounded, probably by our own gunfire. Shortly, I was being assisted by someone who knew doctoring and we were getting the women calmed down some. Mostly they were happy to see any kind of white man, which was enough to tell me that as frantic as they were, if I didn't find Ellie and James here and now, well, they were probably dead. If the Comanche were riled about what had happened at Council House to their own people, it didn't seem unlikely that they wouldn't simply do away with some of their own hostages. I reckon that in a way it was a surprise to see these women alive at all.

I was anxious to find out what I could and move on or go back, so I started to question the women while they were still being tended to.

"Lady," I said, approaching one woman who had a terrifying look in her eyes, "I got to ask you some questions. There's some things I need to know."

"Can't it wait?" the man doing the doctoring said. "These women are pretty bad off."

"No, it can't," I said between grit teeth. I was in a hurry and I was mad and now wasn't a good time to cross me, no matter who you were. "Ma'am, are you two the only hostages left? The only ones they had here before we come?"

But all she could do was stare into the distance, and I

had a feeling that the whole experience might have touched her some.

The next woman was answering some questions to another medicine man who was taking care of her, and for a moment my hope rose. Perhaps she knew, perhaps she had seen Ellie and James.

"Ma'am, I need to know something and I'm figuring maybe you can help me."

She had ratty brown hair and wore clothing that was totally disheveled on her body. It was a good guess the Comanch' had been doing things to her.

"I'm looking for a woman and a boy. The woman's a blonde, sorta tall and the boy is three years of age. Have you see anyone like that in this camp before we got here?"

She looked at me, a puzzled expression on her face, then simply said, "No."

That tore it! Damn them, anyways! The bastards had likely killed them early after the raid on Linnville and buried them on the trail or somehow gotten rid of them.

"Ain't that just something, now," Ward said as he approached me. He was surveying the battlefield, looking at the dead bodies with some sort of perverted pleasure. "Damn, but we did 'em in!"

"Is that all you can think of? Killing Indians?"

"Oh, I forgot," he said, the smile still on his face. And the longer it stayed there, the more I was hating it. "Did you find out anything?"

"No."

"Well, maybe they turned 'em loose and they're wandering around out there." It was a halfhearted try at making me feel at ease and I wasn't at all sure that Ward meant it. "Look, Callahan, you rest easy there a minute. I'm gonna get us some coffee made while these boys clean up." Then he was walking off, muttering to himself a congratulatory "Damn, but we whipped 'em."

I was killing mad now and all I could feel was my fists balling up as I wished for a fight—or something—to take out my anger on. I had to do something. Something!

"You said blonde?"

The voice startled me, but when I turned it was the last woman I had spoken to and of a sudden there was a new hope in me.

"Yes, ma'am."

"Did she have a man's hat with her?"

"Yes, ma'am, that's her." Ellie was forever piling her long blonde hair up underneath her hat and I was forever taking her hat off in playful fun. I remembered it well, surprised I hadn't mentioned it first off.

"There were some men here the other day, gruff-looking men."

"Yes, ma'am," I said, feeling my heart skip a beat. "Go on."

"I never seen them before, but my husband told me about such men. They did some trading here and then they left . . . with the woman and child. They had kept her separated once she was captured back there, although I don't know why."

"The men who took them—"

"There were perhaps a dozen."

"And you say you know who they were?"

"I'm not sure, mister. It's just that they reminded me of those men my husband had told me about."

"And what did he call them, ma'am?"

"Comancheros."

Chapter Nine

I passed up Ward's coffee and asked a few more questions of the woman before mounting the grulla and riding hell-for-leather for San Antonio. Hays, McCulloch, and the rest would likely take out after any remaining Comanches and right then I had other matters that were more important. From what the captive woman had said, there had been a dozen of them at most, and I'd be the last to deny that having a few extra guns along would have been a whole lot easier on the mind. Or maybe it was having the people to fire them that would be easier. Hell, I had more than a couple of guns with me now, and I had learned how to fire those Colt's pistols on the run if I had to. But there are some things a man is best suited to himself, and having a couple hundred riders along to raise dust that could be seen a mile or two off was only going to defeat my purpose. So going it alone was how it would be. Besides, they were my family and my responsibility.

As for the Comancheros, I had had a run-in with

them not long after I had met Ellie and Lije Harper, her pa. Word of them was growing throughout Texas and since I had that first run-in they had taken to more than just bartering and trade with the Comanches. These Comancheros, you see, they started out in this land some time back when we were finishing up the Revolution and getting set up as a country our own selves. Mostly they was a mixture of white and Mexican and some breeds throwed in for measure who traded with the Comanche and other plains Indians to make a living. From what I had heard they could be friendly enough, but that one meeting with them a few years back had soured me on any hospitality they might have. Looking and acting tough is one way to buffalo a man into giving you his possessions, but there are others who would fight at the drop of a hat. And I found out that day that Lije Harper was one of them. The Comancheros had demanded our guns, powder, and ball, and the way they were looking at Ellie, I had a hunch they'd want her in the deal, too. They never did get Ellie or our guns. But Lije and me obliged them about the powder and ball. Yup. Gave them every bit of lead we had in our rifles and that Paterson I had. Like Pa said, a faint heart never filled a flush. And the way I was feeling now I did not care if there were a dozen of them I had to go through to get Ellie and James back. What kept me going was the certain knowledge that most of the Comancheros ran their trade in the western part of Texas and out beyond the Texas territory into what was still Mexican-controlled land. For them to be this far east put them in a strange land and that was to my advantage.

Heading for San Antonio would be on the way for where I had in mind agoing, but there was something else at the back of my mind, something else I was going there for, and for the life of me I couldn't root it free.

It was past sundown when I got there. The grulla was more tired than I was and when I took him to the livery, I rubbed him down and gave him extra of everything I could find. He had stood me well for more years than I cared to count, and I took better care of him than I did my own self. In the shape he was in now he would do me little good for the riding I was figuring on, so I would have to round up another mount somewhere. But that could wait until tomorrow. Right now I was needing a meal and some sleep.

I found a table in a cantina that was still open and ordered a meal and some coffee while I waited. Drinking the coffee and being that hungry were the only things keeping me awake or I do believe I would have passed out right at that table.

"Is Joe all right?"

When I looked up, I squinted in disbelief, then nodded. "Yeah, he's doing fine." Before me stood Lotty Ward, a tray in her hand with my meal on it and that same painted smile she had on her face for the customers back in New York.

"I took the job," she said, as though reading my mind, "until you . . . Rangers got back." I could feel the red creeping up my neck again, but Lotty quickly dropped her smiling waitress routine as she sat down across from me. "Did you find her?" she asked, a strange-sounding note of concern in her voice. It was as if she feared for Ellie's life but at the same time was wishing she were no longer a part of my life.

"Not yet," I said and spent the rest of my meal filling her in on what had happened while we were gone. I didn't say much about what the captive woman had told me, only that I was going out again.

"When will you be back?" Lotty asked, that hint of concern in her voice again.

I knew why she was asking and didn't want any part of it, so I just sat there in silence as I finished the last of my meal and drank the rest of my coffee. When I stood up there was a frown on my face that was intended to get across to her what I was feeling, but she was a stubborn woman her own self and only raised an eyebrow as if to say, "My, my, look what you've done."

"When I find her," I said, but this time the annoyance in my voice was for real. "That's when I'll be back, Lotty, when I find her. Not before!" I added through grit teeth. "So don't wait around."

Then I walked on past her out of the cantina and headed for the stable I had left the grulla at to see if he had finished the feed I had set out for him. On the way it crossed my mind that I could not have gone from one extreme to another any quicker than I just had, for here I was leaving a woman who ran hot and cold on what she wanted in a man and could probably not be counted on for more than waiting on tables, and I was heading for that old grulla, who was likely more dependable than most humans I knew.

He was finishing up what was left of his feed when I got to the stable, and Pedro, the man who stood night watch, was readying the grulla for a second helping.

"Is a good mount, Señor Callahan," he said, "one of the best I ever seen." He yawned, slowly covering his mouth with a hand. "Long nights," he said with a shy smile.

"I know what you mean, amigo." And I did, for there was a time long before the Council House Fight when it would not have been necessary to put a guard on the mounts of even the smallest villages. But now things had changed, and that usually meant that people were changing their way of thinking, especially when that change struck so close to home. I dug in my pocket and pulled out a coin, tossing it to Pedro. "Here," I said, "this ought to take care of the feeding and care of the grulla for a week or so. And I ain't got much to do but take care of my horse and gear, so why not get yourself a cup of coffee to stay awake, Pedro. I'll mind the store for an hour or so," I said with a smile.

"You bet, señor," he said on the way out. "And thanks, I take good care of your mount. You see."

I wasn't about to tell him I was getting near exhaustion, but I had found out early from Bowie a decade before that the Mexican people really knew how to take care of their own, and anyone else they took a liking to, when the occasion arose. And Pedro, working a long night shift like he was, knew the value of a horse to his rider, for out here he truly was nothing without his counterpart. I reminded myself to tell Pedro when he got back about the mount I would need the next day and when to get me up.

I was working on the horse with a currycomb when, just for an instant, it crossed my mind that I was maybe getting old. Or was it because I had so much on my mind, was thinking so much of Ellie and how badly I wanted her? Maybe that was why I didn't hear her walking into the stable. But suddenly I knew she was there.

"Pedro said you were watching the place for him," she said from the shadows. It was the taunting voice in her that spoke, the teasing one I had heard before that could promise so much. It was hard for me to figure out what to expect from this woman anymore, but when she stepped out of the shadows I was just a bit surprised that the one lantern that hung at the entrance to the stable produced a figure still clothed. She still wore the long dress and blouse I had seen earlier in the cantina, but I knew that meant nothing for the moment.

"What do you want?" I asked, the irritation coming back into my voice. But there was another urge in me that I was fighting a lot harder than the anger I felt toward her.

"Just to pass the time." The tone in her voice had changed now as she spoke in a conversational tone. She was leading up to something, something I had no wish to admit to myself, something I wasn't all too sure I could stop from happening.

She came closer, a slow, steady walk across the ground, and as she did I noticed it. The blouse had been pulled loose from the skirt and hung freely at her side only because it had also been unbuttoned. It was making me nervous and fearful as a young pup, all at the same time, and I found myself looking about for the currycomb that wasn't in my hand anymore.

"I really had you pegged, Nathan," she said, smiling, knowing full well she had me rattled. "Whenever things aren't going your way, you have to have something to do with your hands. Well, why not put them around me?" She had that knowing smile on her face, like she was reading my mind and I couldn't help it.

"Did I ever tell you what happened to those rattles old Gar had?" I said in one last, desperate attempt to get out of her reach. I spied the mochila draped over the side of the stall and was about to reach for it when she was suddenly standing in front of me.

"Not now, Nathan," she said, putting her arms around

my neck and pulling me down to her. Then she was
kissing me and like it or not I found myself kissing her
back as I slowly moved my hands up her side, underneath the blouse to her back. I wanted to pull her closer
to me, to feel her warmth, but I couldn't. I wanted to,
you understand, but I couldn't. My hand had wandered
over her back and in the wandering had come across
something that was both familiar and strange to me at
once. The touch of it put a feeling of terror in me, for I
knew all too well what it was. It was the thick, coarse
skin left by a scar that my hand was tracing now. And
the terror came from knowing that the scar likely came
from a bullwhip, just like the one I had across my back.
I felt her flinch as my hand ran slowly back down the
scar, neither one of us now interested in romance.

"Where did you get it?" If I was mad now, it wasn't
at Lotty or what she had led me into, but what had
happened to her.

"Please, Nathan," she replied, a pleading smile now
on her face. "Can't we just forget it? Can't we just—"

"Who did it?" I wasn't feeling any calmer and it
showed and she knew it. "Was it Ward?"

A teardrop rolled from the side of her eye as she
slowly shook her head. "I can't talk about it, Nathan, I
just can't." Then she buried her head in my chest and
began to sob like a little girl. I must have held her for
some time, and looking back, I had the feeling that all I
was holding then was a little girl. A helpless child with
not a friend in the world.

It's strange how things fall into place. You could be
fishing or hunting or just plain whittling and something
you've been beating your head against a wall trying to
remember comes to you right out of nowhere. That
happened while I was holding Lotty. I had it in mind

that Ward was the one who laid the leather to her backside and that jarred into my head the reason I had come back to San Antonio, other than to get more powder and ball and a new mount. It was Ward I wanted to check on. He said he had been in the Seminole War and I could recall Sam Walker talking about being there, too, about how he had first test-fired his Paterson pistol in that war. He had been in more than one skirmish down there and I was thinking he might have run into or heard about Sergeant Joseph Ward, who also claimed to have fought the Seminoles. There was something about the man that didn't sit right with me, and Sam Walker might just hold the key to what I was looking for.

When she stopped crying, she was silent for a moment before slowly pushing herself away from me. And in that moment I thought I had learned something about the woman before me, had maybe gotten a better respect for her and understood her more now. I also realized that I had calmed down quite a bit my own self.

"I must look a sight," she said, dabbing at her eyes with one of those little handkerchiefs women produce at such times. I never could figure out where they kept them hid.

"Best to save the watering for the flowers," I said, feeling out of place and now knowing what it was a man should do. It was times like that I wished Finn was there to give me some lessons on those fancy words he used. Then I realized that Pedro would soon be back, so I started to button up her blouse. "Don't want to catch your death," I added as she silently watched me.

"Was it because of the—"

"No," I said, doing my damnedest to sound gentle

and finding it a hard task. "No, Lotty, it wasn't that at all."

"Because there were others, you know . . . others who stopped just like you did when they put their . . . hands . . . there." The last she said looking away, and I could see that she would soon be in tears again and I wasn't certain I could stand that again.

"Put it this way, Lotty," I said, placing my hands on her shoulders and drawing her near. "I've been down the same trail, and I know it's a rough one." She wouldn't understand that, but it was all I could think of at the time. Then we sort of looked at one another for a minute and finally I said, "In another day, and another time . . . well, I would have purely enjoyed your company, Lotty, I really would. You're a beautiful woman, but you see, so is Ellie, and . . ." My voice trailed off about then and standing there, looking at her, I wasn't sure I could bring myself to say it.

"I know, Nathan, she's your wife."

"Yeah. That's what I was trying to say." If it wasn't for the shadows, I do believe the red in my face would have showed up more than it did, and somehow I was glad it was end of day.

"You'll find her, Nathan," she said, taking my hand in hers and squeezing it, this time with a smile on her face. "I know you will."

Then she left, and watching her go, I had a thought that we just maybe helped each other out in that hour.

"Señor Callahan," I heard a faraway voice say. "It is time, señor, it is time."

I rolled over from where I had spread my bedroll in the back of the stable the night before and saw Pedro standing over me, yawning as he spoke. The lantern was out and behind him I could see the first break of day coming over the horizon.

"That's a fact, pard," I said, rolling onto the hay and then folding my bedroll and packing it in. When I got up I gave Pedro a friendly slap on the back. "Gracias, amigo, you did well." Then I headed for the water trough to clear my head.

After Lotty had gone the night before, Pedro had returned from the cantina. I informed him to wake me at sunup and bedded down at the rear of the stable. With as much Indian activity as we had been having, it was a cinch old Jack Hays was going to have his men out on assignments as early as possible, and I wanted to be able to talk to Sam Walker before he lit a shuck for wherever.

I found him out back of the headquarters building, pouring coffee from one of those cauldrons that look big enough to fill the cups of every Ranger and half the volunteers of the force without putting any dent in the contents. The liquid was burning-hot to my lips, but it was just what was needed for taking the early-morning chill off a body. With a biscuit and a piece of thick jerked beef to round off the meal, we spoke for a short time of Sam Colt and his inventions and just how gifted he seemed to be with these revolvers he was putting out.

"You was down in Florida fighting them Seminoles, weren't you, Sam?" I asked, changing the subject as we poured more coffee. I figured it wouldn't be long before the sun was full up and these Rangers would be moving out, so I asked him right out.

"Sure. Why do you ask?"

"Curious," I shrugged, but the look in his eye told me that Sam knew there was more than curiosity in-

volved in my remark. "Run into a fella a while back
that laid claim to being there, too. Thought you might
have heard of him. Name of Ward, Joseph Ward.
Sergeant, I think he was."

Sam squinted and I could see him going back over
his duty rosters from a few years back. Then a frown
came to his face, as if he were unsure, as he said, "Big
man, thick-set with a hostile tint to his skin?"

"Yeah, that's the one." Now I was getting somewhere.

"If it's him, he wasn't a sergeant when I knew him.
The man I knew was a lieutenant, and if I recall right,
he could fight from sunup to sundown on anybody's
terms . . . and most times win."

I nodded. "That's him," I said, remembering the
run-ins I had had with him not that long ago. "Know
him well?"

Sam shrugged. "Mostly by reputation. The times I
did work with him, the man did his job, but I never
took much of a liking to him."

"How come?"

Sam smiled and finished his coffee. "Like I said,
mostly reputation." When I cocked an eye toward him,
he continued. "Oh, he did his job, all right. Sometimes
too well, I'd say, and I wasn't alone in that line of
thought, Nate. When he wasn't killing Seminoles, he
kept to himself, a loner, I reckon.

"Rumor had it sometime later that he had gotten into
some kind of trouble with the army, but no one was
clear just what it was or with who. If he's a sergeant
now, then I'd say it sounds like he got busted . . .
probably for insubordination. That'd be his style."

"Didn't he have a family?"

"He got mail regular." Sam chuckled, adding, "When
it came in. Come from someplace up north, although I

never paid much attention to it. Why do you ask? Is he causing you trouble?''

''I ain't for sure yet, Sam. But from what I've seen of him, he sure does have a heap of something bothering him inside.'' I gulped the last of my own coffee and looked Sam square in the eye. ''And just between you and me, hoss, I ain't growing too fond of being around when whatever it is that's burring him explodes. I got a hunch that'd be about as healthful as being on the working end of a Hawken with a plugged-up barrel.''

I was right about Hays. A rider had come in the night before with word from Hays and, according to Sam Walker, the orders were to take his men and scout due north of the town. Hays would meet Walker and his men and together they would pursue the renegade Comanches as far as they could. Me, I had other plans. I was heading north by west, and it wouldn't be half as slow as Jack Hays and his boys were going. Somewhere out there I figured I'd find me those Comancheros that had Ellie and James as they made their way back to west Texas or Mexico. Odds were they could sell both Ellie and James to one of the many traders who were making their way to Santa Fe and the surrounding area. And the thought of that didn't please me at all.

I spent the rest of the morning with Pedro, picking out a decent mount to take with me and molding more bullets for both my Colts and the Hawken. There were times, carrying that extra weight, that the Hawken felt cumbersome, but it was the most reliable of any long gun I had ever used, and for what I had in mind I was going to need every edge I could get.

I rode out at noon with nothing but a fresh mount, the Hawken and a brace of Colts. And some hope. Finn would have called it being long on guts and short on sense, but I called it mad and that was enough. I knew what I was riding into and I knew what I was going to have to do, but damn it, I had been too many years without someone like Ellie to sit by and let someone take her from me. Or James, either. Every man wants a heritage, and it's usually that firstborn son he puts so much stock in to carry on his name. And that's what I was feeling when I rode out. If it made a man feel he was too mean to die, then so be it.

'Cause I'll tell you, friend, right about then I was figuring I could fight a grizzly bear, cut his liver out, and feed it to him while he died! And that's mean!

Chapter Ten

Some people never listen. You can beat the hell out of them, cuss them, even threaten them, and they just don't listen. I remember Pa saying that to me as a youngster when he was trying to get us kids to mind him more than we were. It stuck in my mind until a few years later when I was somewhere between hay and grass and I heard him add under his breath, "Thank God, there are still some men like that left." Now, looking at the dust gathering on the horizon as I glanced at my back trail, I wasn't all that sure I agreed with what Pa had said.

It was my second day out and, like Bowie had taught me, I was taking a look at my back trail. It was the first time I had cause to go this far west in the territory, and in a strange land, it paid to stop every so often and give your mount a breather while you took in the landscape around you. "Always watch your back trail" was one of the first rules you learned right quick in a land as big as this one. When Bowie first told me that I had asked him why and he said, "Things always look different when you are going in the opposite direction." From then on I did it out of habit. And a good habit it was, for what I spotted was someone trailing me. Whether on purpose or by accident I did not know, but I had a suspicion it wouldn't be long before I found out.

I rode a bit farther, a few miles perhaps, before I spotted a waterhole. The water was good and the horse and I did a fair bit of drinking. It was late afternoon and chances of finding another hole like this one anywhere near were slim, so making camp seemed about the most sensible thing to do. And I would have set to it, were it not for the dust cloud on the horizon.

At first it crossed my mind that Walker had sent some of his men to give me a hand. I had given him a brief outline of what I had in mind doing and he knew as well as I that for a man alone it was an all but impossible task. But he also knew that I would try it regardless of that knowledge. Then I noticed that the dust was coming from more of a southerly than eastern direction and felt the pit of my stomach knot up like a lead ball. It was the kind of feeling you get when you know something is going to happen and that there ain't a hell of a lot you can do about it.

"You were right, Pa," I heard myself saying as I squinted at what looked to be the outlines of Joe and Lotty Ward. "Some people never listen. Damn him, anyway!" I wasn't sure whether I was cussing Joe Ward or Sam Walker or both. Suddenly, I remembered Walker mentioning a rider from Hays's camp coming in the night before with his orders. There was no reason to suspect it had been Ward, but that would be the only explanation I could think of that would bring both him and his wife out after me.

It also put a change in my plans. I was madder than hell at Ward for what he had done to Lotty and that would have been my first order of business once I got Ellie and James back safely. Now, with him here, there would be no getting around it. I wanted a clear mind when I went after those Comancheros, a task that would be hard enough without the temptation to take on Ward first. Better to get it over with and be rid of the man, I told myself. But how I would do it, I didn't know.

There was some deadwood in the vicinity but more would be needed, so I was sitting in the saddle when the two of them rode up.

"You got a good horse there, Callahan," Ward said, riding up beside me. He seemed to be in the same jovial mood I had left him in after the fight at Plum Creek and it didn't improve on the way I was feeling one bit. Ward didn't notice it, by now getting used to seeing me scowl at him, but there was more fear in Lotty's face than I had ever seen in a woman before. If she sensed what I had in mind, then she was doing her best to hide it. "Took me the better part of two days to catch up with you."

"I got a good rifle, too," I said, looking first at Ward, then at my Hawken. I put the rifle to my shoulder, pointing toward the sky as though to test its aim, then glanced down the right and left sides of the barrel. "Only one problem with it."

"What's that?" Ward was still enjoying himself, a half smile on his face, while inside I was learning to hate him the more.

"Got caught afoot in a raid one time," I said, trying to sound as ordinary as I could. "Run out of ammunition and an Injun come at me on his horse. Well, I swung this Hawken at him and hit him flush in the gut, see? He was gone beaver after that fight, but ever since then I been shooting just a hair to the left of my targets.''

"Better get it fixed," Ward said, a serious look on his face now. "You know how it is without a good weapon out here."

"Oh, I intend to get it fixed," I said. "Right now."

As I said it I was swinging the Hawken full force to my right, just clearing the top of the head of his horse as I did. The barrel hit him full in the chest, high enough to send him clean out of his saddle in a somersault over the horse's rear. He hit the ground with a thud as I slid off my own mount and I knew I had him. I wasn't about to throw down the Hawken, for the sand and dirt would gum up the works so badly it would take a full day to get it back in working order, and I didn't have time like that to waste. He was just getting up when I got him in view, so I rammed the barrel of the rifle into his gut, pushing him back. He coughed some, then tried to straighten up so's to take a swing at me. I waited until he was standing tall and brought the thick butt of the Hawken up into his midsection right below the breastbone. All of a sudden the wind flew out of him and he was bending forward again as I brought my knee up into his face and he rolled to the side.

"You're real good at taking after women, ain't you, Ward?" I said, throwing the business end of the rifle down into his stomach. He had a shocked, puzzled look on his face, as though he couldn't understand what I had done, but for what I had in mind, pure terror would be more in order. "I could kill you where you are, Ward, and not feel a thing watching you take three days to die."

"What the devil—"

I pulled back the hammer on the rifle, the muzzle still resting on the man's stomach.

"No! No! Stop it!" came the scream behind me. "It's not him, Nathan, it's not *him*!!" she screeched, and the first thing that ran through my mind was that it wouldn't be long before we had a good share of the Indian population in the area in either for supper or to make supper out of us.

"What do you mean, it's not him?!"

"It's not him," she said, a bit more calmly, tears in her eyes as she looked away.

"But you said—"

"I never said, Nathan. I—"

Then she was crying with that little white handkerchief in her hand. And I remembered that she was right. She hadn't said who had given her the scars, only that she could not talk of it. And I don't mind telling you that made me feel like one damned fool if ever there was one. I had automatically figured it was Ward, since he was the man she was married to. The thought that it might have been someone else never crossed my mind. But then, I never was much good with women anyway.

"Get up, Ward," I said, the anger in my voice directed more at my own self than at the man before me or what he might or might not have done. "I'm gonna need firewood, so get on your horse. You and me are gonna get some . . . and we're gonna talk."

As we rode out of camp, it became evident that Ward was more confused at what was going on than he was at my having beaten him. We rode in silence at a slow walk for a time before we spotted some deadwood scattered here and there. I still had the Hawken draped across the saddle and pointed at Ward's midsection.

"You mind pointing that somewhere else? Makes me

nervous." He was trying to be humorous about it, which was more than I could say for me, but at least you had to give the man credit for trying.

We ground-tied the horses and started gathering loose pieces of wood. There didn't seem to be much bothering Ward, probably because he knew I was the one that needed to do the explaining. And being in that kind of position will put a crimp in any man's style. Like always, I figured it was best to get it over with.

"You much on listening, Ward," I said, meeting his glance for the first time since dismounting.

"Yeah," he said, a grin starting to appear on his face. "I guess you could say I've done my share. That is, when I ain't talking."

"In that case, hoss, there's some things you ought to know. And maybe some things I ought to know, too. If you know what I mean."

Ward nodded and I told him about Lotty and the advances she had made at me and how I had tried to put them off, from that first night to the one at the stable only a few days ago. In the telling, I made sure I stayed my distance from Ward, for I did not trust his actions, as jealous as he was. The man was big and perhaps a bit slow, but once he got going it would be hard to stop him. I found myself on the lookout for some surprise move, some motion that would indicate he was going on the warpath. Yet, when I was finished, I was surprised more at how calm he had remained throughout the telling of it all.

"It's nothing I haven't known about or suspected," he said by way of explanation. "I reckon she's teased more men than I'll ever know about," he continued, a complacent, almost satisfied look coming to his face.

"But you've got to figure, Callahan, that I know one thing that the rest of you don't."

"What's that?"

His face broadened to a grin as he said, "She ain't gonna do no more than just tease you." Now I was the one feeling confused, for what he had just said sounded little like the truth from my side of the creek. True, Lotty might have been luring me on at the first, but the night in the stable sure did stand out as one real attempt to do something about my marriage status. But if Ward wanted to believe otherwise, then so be it. I wasn't about to spoil the man's vision of the world as he saw it just so I could get my face busted in.

"I don't understand," I said, even if I did have a notion that I did.

"Look, Callahan," he said, all seriousness now. "I know why you jumped me back there, and I can't say as I blame you, because I'd have done the same thing. But you've got to believe something. I really love that woman, Callahan, I really do. I ain't never laid a hand on her or beat her or nothing. Oh, I've cussed at her and all, but drunk or sober, I never done *nothing* to her. Especially what you found on her back." At first he sounded like a desperate man trying to persuade me of what must seem the impossible. But when he stopped there was a look about him as though he had discovered something so simple he had overlooked it at the start.

"Tell me something, Callahan, just what makes that scar so interesting to you, other than the body it's on?"

"This." I pulled out my shirt, reached over a shoulder and pulled it up, baring my back. Ward let out a whistle of disbelief when he saw the jagged scar that ran from my left shoulder to the bottom of my right side. It was two inches thick in places, I was told. Not that it mattered, for the pain of its memory was worse than any of the healing pain could ever have been. "It's a long story, Ward, but I'll guarantee you, it's one I'll never forget."

"Can't fault you for that," he said as I tucked my shirt back in my pants. It was an awkward moment for the both of us as he paused before continuing.

"It was almost three years ago when I met her, just after the war was over. I courted her and after a while we got married and I got stationed in New York." He paused a moment and it could have been a shy young boy I saw before me who was turning beet-red in the face. He looked away as he said, "I know it's hard to believe from the way I act, but I was more gentle with her than I ever was with anyone. I was wanting a family and . . . well, you know how that is. A man wants a son to take on his name. But, Lotty"—he shrugged, helplessly—"she couldn't. It wasn't that she couldn't bear children, you understand. It's that she wouldn't. I reckon that's when I started to drink more than usual."

"You mean she refused you? Like she done all the rest?"

"I reckon you could say that. Not that I blame her." There was a sad look on his face now and I knew he was going back to a memory as painful to him as the scar on Lotty's back. "She had that scar on her back when I first met her," he said softly. I was getting the notion it was harder for him to say it than think it, but he did just the same. "And all the pain that went with it, I reckon."

"But if you didn't do it, then who—"

"Her father," he said, a meanness coming out in the man I had not seen before. "It was her father that done

it to her . . . after he raped her!'' There was a fire in
his eyes, and a bit of madness, too, I thought. His face
turned livid and suddenly a clenched fist was shaking
before me. "But I got him, Callahan, I got him!''

"Easy, Ward. Just . . . take it easy, hoss.'' There
was no way in God's green earth I was going to contra-
dict the man now. There was the look of death in his
eyes and I knew that if he were pushed to it, death
would spread to the nearest thing in reach. "How did
you do it?'' I asked, more to change the subject than
out of interest.

He was silent for a moment, reaching back in his
tortured memory again for the details. "We had maneu-
vers that first year of our marriage. I knew where he
lived and made a trip there on a pass one weekend. He
was a miserable old man, Callahan, and I got to him. I
made him pay for every bit of pain he ever done to
Lotty, every bit. With my bare hands.''

With that last his voice trailed off and the strength
seemed to leave the man as his eyes glazed over the
distance. I could imagine how it must have been, the
fury in Ward easily overcoming the old man as he beat
him to death. Seeing him now, I knew that he wasn't
right, that a part of him had snapped along the way.
And I wondered if his drunken violence might not have
come from the reliving of that nightmare each time he
fought himself and that bottle. I had seen the same kind
of agonizing look on Bowie's face years ago, could tell
it was the thought of his own family dying that brought
it on. Worse, I knew as well as anyone that there was
nothing a body could do but wait for it to pass, hope for
it to pass. I always thought that toward the end, while
we were fighting that revolution back in '35 and '36,
Jim Bowie had welcomed death. Too many of us, his

friends, had seen him willingly lay his life on the line simply to fight, to give the devil one more chance to take him. Seeing Ward now, I had the feeling that same death wish was haunting him as well.

"I told Lotty I had seen him and talked to him and that he'd never bother her again," he said, coming back to the present. "She can't know no different, Callahan."

"She won't," I said, knowing what he meant.

Like Lije Harper said one time, conversation sort of dried up after that, and we gathered up the remaining deadwood and returned to camp in silence.

Lotty made the meal and it was getting on to sunset when we ate, but the way she kept looking up at Ward and me I had the feeling she might be believing in miracles, what with the way me and Ward had started out rowdy and come back from our wood gathering about as tame as a wore-out bronc. And she might not have been far off, for it seemed that Ward had done a complete change in a matter of minutes. I had no idea what had caused it, but if getting it out of his system was what was needed, I was all for it. No man ever takes a liking to admitting that he's wrong, and I knew good and well that a man like Ward—at least the man I had first met—wasn't going to let a moment pass without shoving it down my throat. But the man before me now, well, he seemed more at ease with himself and sort of comfortable with the world to boot, something I had not yet seen in Joe Ward. But then, that was nature for you—changeable.

We ate in silence and I don't think none of the three of us was wanting to be the first one to start talking. It seemed evident to me that neither Ward nor his wife knew what to say to each other just then. And me, well,

I wasn't sure if anything I could say to them would be the right thing. Still, it had to be done, and when you got right down to it, there was only one reason I had come out this way, and it was still heavy on my mind.

"Not much of a trail out here," I said, sipping my coffee. "Least, the one I'm looking for." That didn't get much of a response from anyone, so I tried what Finn called the direct approach. Hell, for me it was the *only* approach! "You never did say what brought you out in this direction . . . after me."

"Long story," Ward said, looking across the fire over his own cup.

I shrugged. "I got all night."

"You know me, Callahan, just looking for another fight."

He said it with the hint of mischief in his voice I had grown used to and I thought to myself, Yes, I am, Ward. . . . I'm getting to know you real well.

"If you say so," I said, shrugging again.

"Do you know what you're up against?" Lotty asked, finally speaking up.

"Far as I can figure, it's somewhere around a half dozen Comancheros."

"Well, now, ain't that just a bit outnumbered for one man alone?" Ward asked.

"Some might think so," I said as a slow smile came to my face. "But I don't." As I said it I glanced down at the butts of the two Colts in my waist. Right about then I probably looked about as mad as Ward had earlier and I doubted he figured a man could have the faith in the machinery of Sam Colt as much as I did, but I did. I surely did. Given the right edge, I was figuring it was only going to take one of my pistols to do in those Comancheros and get Ellie and James back.

If they died hard, I might have to use the second Colt, but one way or another I was getting my wife and son back. "Besides," I added, "a man's got to do what he's got to do."

"Yeah, there's that." Ward nodded.

That was something a man learned real fast when he left home and went out on his own. Especially on the frontier. You did what you had to to get by and there was no second thought about it; you simply did it. Whether it was killing meat for the fire or some intruder who decided he liked your gear or outfit or guns or land as much as you did and wanted to take it from you. Whether you saved someone's life by putting your own in danger or had your bacon pulled out of the fire by someone else. It happened. You did it and got on with it. And unless you were some young buck who figured he had to impress everyone by bragging about his exploits, or unless you were one of the old-timers who did most of the storytelling, well, odds were you never made much of it. Others would likely spread the word and, like Sam Walker said, it would become a part of your reputation. Finn had all sorts of flowery words those writers and historians he read about used to describe all of it. But the way I figured, most of us that were doing anything close to what Finn's writers described were too damned tired after the doing to worry much more about anything but getting on with it. It was one of the things a man learned early in life, and when he had to say it, it was seldom a man he was saying it to that didn't understand him. It was the way of things.

Ward looked to all of his sides, taking in the total barrenness of the area before it disappeared into the night.

"Looks like another part of nowhere that I ain't seen yet."

"You're right about that," I admitted. It was the first time I had been this far west in the territory and from what I had seen the past two days, it was the kind of land that got sparse right quick. The eastern part of Texas had good graze and farm land, but riding as far as I had in the last two days, I wouldn't have been surprised at all to learn that someone had been out here and taken one look at it and figured that maybe God forgot about it when He did His creating.

"Stay out here long enough, I reckon a man would get a real good idee of what that Columbus fella was going through," Ward said. Then, picking up a handful of sand, he let it sift through his fingers, adding, "But he had water."

"I found a man who had been out this way a time or two before I left. He was kind of sketchy about the lay of the land, but from what I've seen so far I don't think I'd blame him too much. Claimed the few trails there are out here get blown away with the wind or washed out by flash floods. But there's a couple or three of them out here that carry the same name, it seems, and once you find it it's followable." I paused a moment, swallowed the remainder of my now cold coffee, and looked at Ward, then Lotty. "You sure you want a hand in this game? It don't look like it'll get any better afore it gets worse."

"Like you said, Callahan," Ward said, a finality in his voice, "there's things a man's got to do."

"Does this trail have a name?" Lotty asked.

"So they say. They call it the Comanche Trail."

Now, there are some things you can say that will dry up a conversation as fast as the hot sun in a drought and the mention of Indians back then was one of them. When I said it, I saw Lotty visibly shudder and it ran through my mind that she was likely a whole lot more scared of the hostiles right then than she would ever be of those rattles old Gar took off'n those snakes.

The sun was down and we would have a long ride ahead of us tomorrow, so we all turned in.

Chapter Eleven

The best time to make tracks—or follow them—in a land like this was to do it in the early-morning hours before the sun got high and slowed you down just by the purely hellish amount of heat it put out. So we were up before daylight and covered a good bit of ground before noon. I wanted to get to Ellie and James in the worst way, but experience told me that I would get there a hell of a lot slower without a horse than with one, so, as I had done the two previous days, most of that afternoon's tracking was done afoot, leading the horses. It wouldn't be until much later in the afternoon that I planned for us to mount up and search out a waterhole to make camp at.

It wasn't long before making dry camp at noon that I ran across what I thought to be the Comanche Trail. I had been heading north by west and this trail veered off directly north, just as that fella back in San Antonio had said it would, which was like I was planning it anyways. The way I figured, those Comancheros were headed

back west to their own stomping grounds after their part
in that raid back at Linnville. And if they wanted to get
back to their roost in one piece, they'd not be traveling
any faster than I had been of late. It was riding that
grulla hell-for-leather to San Antonio that gave me my
edge. I never made any claim to be any kind of a
strategy genius like that Caesar fella Finn spoke of
every now and then, but what I was doing was the only
thing that came to mind when I learned the Comancheros
had my wife and son, so I reckon you might say I was
gambling it would work. Damn it, it had to work! If it
didn't, I would be less one family, and I don't mind
telling you that I had no desire to live through the
experience of my friend Bowie and the agony he had
gone through. So seeing that trail sort of filled me with
a whole new urge to get on with it and catch up with
these renegades.

If there was anything bothering me, it was the presence of Ward and his wife more than the number of
Comancheros I might encounter. Lotty was in a situation where her feminine wiles would do no good at all
and, from the reaction she had given the night before,
was scared to death. And Ward, well, he seemed to
have softened some after confessing what had been on
his mind for some time, apparently, and that might
have been good for the soul but it made me wonder if I
wouldn't have been better off with the old Ward I had
known. At least that man was in a fighting mood all his
waking moments, drunk or sober. From what I had seen
so far today, the man was going through a lot of
looking inside himself and was quieter than I had seen
him thus far. The question I had to ask myself was
whether or not I could count on them when the lead

started flying. And the answer I kept coming up with
was . . .

There was something else that stuck in my craw,
something that Ward had said the night before. It didn't
sound right with what Sam Walker had told me of the
man, so when we broke dry camp and Ward lagged
behind, I pulled up alongside Lotty and decided to find
out the truth of the matter.

"You been with him going on three years now?" I
asked, trying to sound casual, knowing I was likely
talking too hard to sound anything close to it.

"Yes, since '38. Why do you ask?" If she suspicioned
anything, she didn't show it . . . or didn't care.

"Well, a friend of mine says he worked with Ward
back in the Seminole War, and he mentioned that Ward
got regular mail from his family. And I was wondering—"

"If I was the 'family' your friend spoke of?" There
was a hint of disdain in her voice, as though she knew I
were going to ask it.

"Or . . ." I shrugged. If she was that good, let her
fill in the missing blanks her own self; me, I had been
in enough arguments with a woman to know there ain't
no man ever wins one.

"Or that Joe and I haven't told you the whole truth?"
It was beginning to look like I was about to get into one
of those can't-win arguments.

"Well, it just seems—" I cut myself short again,
found myself coughing, but it wasn't any sand in my
throat that was making me do it. It was the kind of
feeling you get when you're walking through the woods
in the winter and accidentally upset a bear that's hiber-
nating in a tree trunk. You don't know whether to shoot
him and take a chance on making him that much madder,
or run like hell, knowing that it's likely to have the

same effect on him. For me it's like that with women. I just can't win.

"Tell me something, Nathan. Why do you think Joe and I followed you out here? Why do you think we came?"

There's times that people get backed into a corner about something they don't really want to talk about. And no matter how hard they think about it, they never do seem to find the right thing to say, so what they usually wind up saying is one word that makes them feel like a fool, despite how things could turn out. And that's what I said. "Well . . ."

"The truth, Nathan." She said it evenly, which was not at all what I expected.

"You sure?" I frowned.

"Yes, Nathan," she replied with a smile that reminded me a lot of Ellie's, maybe because I got the feeling it was genuine. "I'm sure."

"Well, to tell you the truth, Lotty, I had a feeling that you and Ward might have been after that shipment of guns I was taking back to Texas, even after you stepped in with those highwaymen. Then, after I seen how much Ward enjoyed killing people, it crossed my mind that he was an out-and-out troublemaker. I've seen more than my share of them out here. But now"—I glanced back at Ward, who was still quiet, still minding his own business—"I ain't sure what to expect.

"You see, Lotty, this is one helluva gamble I'm taking and if you and he deal yourselves in . . . well, if you don't have a pat hand, you'd better be able to bluff like hell and stay to the end. If you can't look 'em straight in the eye, even with a losing hand . . ."

"I understand." She said it softly, putting a soft hand over mine and gently squeezing it before letting go. And I mean to tell you, it rattled me. It wasn't at all what I expected, but then I was finding out that Lotty Ward was an uncommon woman.

"You were wrong about the first part," she said after a brief silence. "Joe would never have stolen anything from you." For a moment I saw a smile form on her lips as she continued. "A bottle of whiskey, perhaps, but never anything else. Not even a woman. He's a hard man to get used to and even harder to understand, as I'm sure you well know by now. But believe me, Nathan, somewhere inside of him he has a sense of values. He simply never shows them.

"You said something about letters during the war. Well, your friend was right. Joe did have a family and he did get mail regularly while he was away from home. Until the letters stopped and one day he received one from a friend telling him that his family had been killed in an Indian raid. Some senseless incident that just . . . happened." I thought I saw the beginnings of a tear form in her eyes as she looked at me and said, "He had a son, you know. He was about the age of your boy, I believe.

"I don't think it's the killing itself that he likes, Nathan, I honestly don't. It's just that it brings back to him what happened and you've seen what that does to him."

"Yeah," I said, knowing what she meant. "I've seen the madness in his eyes more than a time or two."

"He would have gone on with those other Rangers if he hadn't heard about your wife and son. Yes, he'll fight for you, Nathan."

"Are you sure?"

She was silent again, going over a moment of thought in her mind before she looked up at me. "Do you remember what you said last night about what a man has to do?''

''Yes.''

''Well, he'll never admit it to you, and don't you dare ask him, but keeping your family from winding up the way his did . . . well, that's what Joe Ward 'has to do.' ''

In a way it made sense and I could understand it. I had felt the same rage when I found out that Bowie had died at the Alamo, the same sense of revenge that Ward must have felt about his wife and son. And if it was anything like the vengefulness I felt, it probably didn't matter to Ward that he was going up against a stacked deck. But Lotty coming along . . . well, this wasn't a place for waiting on tables or anything else ladylike I knew of.

''Why did you come?''

''Let's just say I decided I want to meet your wife,'' she said with that same smile. Then, in a more serious tone, she added, ''Besides, he's my man.''

Chapter Twelve

We rode in silence the rest of the afternoon until I figured it was time we start looking for a waterhole rather than just tracking. I mounted up and looked forward out of habit, and it's a good thing I did. Being in the saddle and standing on the ground can have as much effect on what a man sees as watching his own back trail does. And it was that difference I spotted when I got on my mount. At least, it looked like it.

"Ward," I said, not taking my eyes off the horizon. When the man came forward, I had him mount up. "My eyes ain't as good as they used to be. Tell me if I'm seeing things out there or is that maybe a horse and rider heading west?"

Ward squinted, nodded. "No mistaking it. And if he stops, you can bet it's a campfire I see the beginnings of not far from him." When he spoke next there was a frown on his face. "What do you think?"

"I think I found what I'm looking for." I dismounted and handed my reins to Lotty. "One way or another, you and me are gonna find out." Then, before she could say anything, I turned to Lotty. "You hang on to these horses. Sit tight until we get back."

"But what do I—"

"As long as you don't hear any shooting, you're safe."

"And if I do?"

"Get on your horse and get the hell outta here."

"We'll be back," Ward said, kissing her on the forehead. His reassurance calmed her some and I felt better about knowing the horses would be here when we got back.

They couldn't be but a few miles from us and more than likely were probably travelers or traders heading for Santa Fe. But to be sure, I led us around to the east side of their camp. At least when we approached, the sun wouldn't aid in pointing us out to them—whoever they were.

Most men who had been drinking as long and as hard as Ward had would have lost their reflexes as well as their innards by now, so I was kind of surprised to see the ex-sergeant keep up the pace I set as we neared the camp.

There was a small gully that enabled us to get as close as a hundred yards to the camp, but any closer would risk being seen by them and I wasn't ready for that. Not yet.

"Damn!" I said, underneath my breath.

"What's the matter?" Ward whispered.

"Can't see nothing from here."

Without a word, Ward dug inside his coat pocket, producing a short bulky piece of metal I had never seen before. Then he pulled out one end of it, extending its length and placing it up against his eye.

"What in the hell is that?"

"Spyglass" was all he said as I watched him move it from left to right, then back left again. "Brings in your game so's they look bigger far away." I wasn't sure I understood what he was talking about, but it didn't matter once I heard him speak again. "Your wife a yellow-haired woman with a son, three, four years old with the same kind of hair?"

"Yes," I said, feeling something jump in me at the same time I reached for Ward's spyglass. "How do you work this thing?"

When he explained, he said, "Sight in on the left side of camp, over by a couple of mules and what looks like boxes of contraband or something."

It took a while to find them and not even the amazement at being able to see a body so far off look so close could take a hold of me. All I was wanting was to see Ellie and James alive and breathing. And that they were. Ellie's hat was gone, but she and the boy looked to be all right from what I could see, although it looked as if they both had their hands bound behind them with rope or rawhide to keep them from escaping. I wanted in the worst way to run up to them and get them out of there, get them away from those renegades. I must have started to make a fist, for the next thing I knew, Ward was taking the spyglass from my hand.

"Easy now, pard," he said. "Don't go getting too excited. There's just the two of us, you know."

"Yeah. Sure." Suddenly I was feeling a combination of relief and terror all at once, knowing in the back of my mind that it would not leave me until my wife and son were free . . . or I was dead trying to make them that way. Seeing them, even from this distance, was enough to make me forget about the ache in my bones and exhaustion I was feeling. It didn't seem possible, but for the better part of ten days now I had been riding, tracking or fighting somebody, and I wasn't sure how much farther I could go. One thing I determined in my mind right then and there was that I would do whatever I had to to get Ellie and James out of that camp. And to do that meant one thing to me. I'd have to find something to do, something to keep me occupied so I wouldn't have time to think, for a man that set to thinking could be dangerous to you. In a situation like this he'd likely either lose his fight or get to thinking nothing could stop him, and too much of either one was bad to my mind.

"Got any ideas?"

"Not yet," I said, watching the sun readying to set. "One thing's for sure, though."

"What?"

"We're gonna have to take 'em at night or just afore sunrise if we're to get Ellie and James and *us* out of this in one piece."

Ward nodded and we headed back to Lotty and the horses. When we got there, she seemed relieved to see us and went about making what she could of a meal for us. We couldn't afford to start a fire of our own lest we give away our position, so the meat was cold and the water was warm and the biscuits were hard. I had been in worse situations and eaten less food before and figured that Ward had, too, for he did little complaining. Lotty even seemed to adjust to the lack of niceties most women favored.

It's strange how you can get between a rock and a hard spot and it'll be looking like you're never going to make it, and all of a sudden the back of your mind will bring back a memory of something that was right funny at the time. I never could figure out why that is, but I've a notion it's a mixture of your mind playing tricks on you and a desperate man's wiles being throwed all into one. Whatever it was, it put a thought in my mind that sat there for a minute and sort of grew. And the more I thought of it, the more I figured it would work. Yep, it might just. Hell, it had to!

"Callahan?"

"What?" I asked, coming out of my reverie.

"You're starting to bother me," Ward said, a frown on his face. When I cocked an eye at him, he continued. "You've got a smile on your face that reminds me of the town fool just before he got hit by lightning."

"Oh," I said and smiled again. "I was just thinking."

"Well, if you want to get them out of there," he said, throwing a thumb over his shoulder, "you better be concentrating on more serious things."

I never was too good at making sense of why people feel the way they do; that was Finn's handle on figuring. He was a real thinker, that one. He could sit down and tell you why a man did this or the other after he got through studying him or reading about him in one of his books. Me, if I could see it I'd tell you just what was going to happen and maybe how. But figuring out my own feelings went about as far as how I felt about my wife and son and Finn and the rest of my family and close friends. But of a sudden I had a notion that everything would turn out right and that the situation wasn't as bad as it seemed. Part of it was the thought of having Ellie and James free and with me, which had been a constant thought for some time now. The other, like I said, was something I could see. It was Ward. When he had spoken to me just then, the surliness in his voice had returned and so had the tough, demanding sergeant in him. And for that I was glad.

"You know, Ward, my brother is always telling me 'bout how I'm collecting things and never throwing 'em away. How the only things worth saving are them books of his."

"Callahan, this ain't no time to be reminiscing." The anger and impatience in his voice were building and I knew I had the old Ward back.

"Lotty, you remember old Gar, that fella I was telling you about that killed all them snakes?"

She shuddered at the mention of them. "Please, Nathan, I'm trying to forget them."

"Callahan, you ain't making no sense! None a-tall!" The fire was building in him, but he was getting a bit too loud, so I held up my hand for silence as I got up and walked over to my horse and the mochila draped across its back.

I dug inside the mochila and pulled out a fistful of rattles from old Gar's snakes. I was still smiling and still had the two of them wondering as I tossed the rattles into the sand at Lotty's feet. If it had been hard rock, they would have made a bit of a sound, but as they were, just the sight of them scared her and she jumped back.

"What the hell did ya do that for?" Ward asked, although he, too, had gotten skittish at the sight of the rattles. "You know what she said about those damn things."

"Most people ain't too keen on rattlesnakes, me included, especially when they're alive," I said, picking up the rattles. "Fact is, all most people got to do is hear those rattles and they know for a fact that they'd better git out'n that area."

"You ain't thinking—"

I nodded, my grin widening. "Yup. These are gonna buy us some time to get Ellie and the boy out of that camp."

The only reason I slept that night was out of exhaustion. I was certain we could pull off our surprise party and get away with it, but even being that keyed up couldn't keep me from sleep.

Before we turned in, Lotty proved that women are as much in the habit of packing away bits and pieces as men are when she found some thread and set to tying those rattles together in a few pairs.

It seemed like I had just fallen asleep when someone was giving me a nudge in the side. When I opened my eyes, I could see Ward standing against a fading moon. It must have been a couple, three hours before daylight, so we had plenty of time to get there and do some checking around.

I had outlined what we needed to do the night before, so we saddled our mounts and rode out in silence, following the same route Ward and I had taken the first time. We were only halfway there when we dismounted and walked the horses to the same gully we had visited the previous day, this time walking them slowly to the west side of the camp. Thinking on it, it seemed to be to our advantage to have Ellie and James located on the west side of camp at that. Approaching them from the east side of camp at daylight would make us stick out like a gopher at a rattlesnake convention. Coming in from the west side, they wouldn't see us with any luck. And as much as I wanted my wife and son back, and as much as I was figuring Ward wanted to fight, we were still going to need all the edge we could get.

We ground-tied the horses so they'd be ready when
we were and I said a silent prayer. Likely Ward and
Lotty had their own mounts and knew what they were
good for. Me, I had what amounted to a replacement
for my grulla and had no idea of whether the horse
would stand his ground or turn tail and run at the sound
of gunshots. And it was a certainty that shots would be
fired, of that I was sure.

Lotty's part in this fandango would be largely what
Finn called a diversion. The plan called for her to move
up behind one of the several stacks of boxes situated
throughout the camp and toss in some of those rattles
and give a tug at her line to them, just like she were
fishing. Ward was to cover the far side of the camp
where the horses and mules were located and see if he
could find one that was free to cut loose when the
shooting started. But it was those boxes that made me
nervous as I studied them, and Ward must have noticed
it.

"What's the matter?"

"Something don't look right," I said. "For a catch
saddle outfit, they sure do look like they're taking it a
mite too easy. I was them, I'd keep some of those
mules loaded and ready to go. But everything's stacked
up, boxes and such all over the place. It just don't look
right."

"Probably decided to rest for a day or two," Ward
said, and when it didn't ease the frown on my face, he
added, "It'll make it that much easier for us to get in
and out without getting followed by the whole of them."

"Could be, but it still don't look right."

If it hadn't been for the moon, we would have had to
wait until daybreak to raid the camp. As it was there
was still an hour or so until first light, the moon giving

us just enough light to pot shot these buzzards without making too awful much of a shadow our own selves.

I never had occasion to try sleeping on hard ground with my hands tied behind my back, but I never could figure it for one of the most comfortable of positions. Which is why Ellie and the boy were awake when I spotted them. There was a heavyset guard leaning on one of the crates next to Ellie and James, passing the late night by counting the stars or his wishes or some damn thing. Put it this way. He weren't too attentive.

One good thing about being in that much sand was that it made it that much easier to sneak up on them without making any noise. So far everything was going right. But then I stepped out from behind the boxes to Ellie's side.

And James saw me.

"Daddy!" he yelled out.

I had the bowie in one hand and the Colt in the other. With one swift slice, I cut the bonds on both Ellie and James, at the same time hearing what sounded like a cry of "Snakes!" to one side of the camp. Ellie was as surprised as James and for an instant simply stood there in awe. And she damn near died!

The guard had grabbed for his own rifle and was bringing it to bear on Ellie when I heard Ward's old army rifle boom and the man pitched forward over the boxes, a chunk of meat tearing open the front of his shirt as the bullet exited.

"There's hosses down in the gully!" I yelled to Ellie. "Now git!"

As Ellie grabbed James and ran out of sight, I saw Ward hit one of the camp members with the butt of his rifle. Several over near Lotty were shooting at the rattles in all the confusion. But they weren't all fooled, for two more near the campfire had pulled out horse pistols when they saw me. I snapped off a shot at one as the other pulled the trigger of his own gun and I felt something jerk at my left shoulder. The second shot from the Colt hit him in the chest and if he wasn't dead he damn sure ought to have been.

"Get out of here, Callahan!" I heard Ward yell from the other side of the fire. "Damn it, git!" One of the banditos hit him in the chest with his own rifle butt and the man fell backwards. I fired one more shot, hitting the man who had knocked Ward down, and left in one big hurry.

I was heading for the horses when, out of the corner of my eye, I saw Lotty running from her own position. We were halfway there when she stumbled and fell. I stopped for an instant, waiting for her to get back up, but she didn't. I glanced at the gully, then back at the camp where they were starting to get organized now, then ran to Lotty. She had a pained look on her face and was bleeding from a wound high in her back.

I fired another shot at one Comanchero who'd decided he was brave enough to venture beyond the camp, busting loose some splinters of a box next to him. It made him think better of the idea and he took cover while I picked up Lotty and made my way back to the horses. Ellie and James were mounted double, Ellie handing me the reins of one horse as I hoisted Lotty up into the saddle.

"You're gonna have to ride some, lady," I said, taking in a once rosy-cheeked face now gone white. "Think you can do it?"

She nodded and that was all I needed.

"Point him that-a-way," I told Ellie, sticking my

arm out toward the direction we had come from, "and let's get the hell out of here."

She took the lead and I followed beside Lotty, making sure she stayed in the saddle. Most of the time there was a grim look of pain on her face, but she never uttered a word, not one. She had sand, this one, but I knew what hard riding could do to your insides when you were gun-shot, and even without making a sound, I knew she wouldn't go far without having the bullet taken out first. At least, not without dying. So I urged my mount forward and had Ellie pull up when we reached the dry camp area we had been in the night before.

Lotty grimaced as I took her from the saddle as gently as I could. She was in a bad way and I got the feeling Ellie knew it as much as I did when she saw her.

"She is beautiful" was all Lotty said, taking in Ellie's features.

When Ellie looked up at me all I could think to say was "Some men are lucky." The next thing I knew she was in my arms, saying something into my shirt I could barely make out, squeezing my chest hard enough to remind me that I still had some ribs that needed looking after.

When she stood back, her eyes widened as she saw the blood on my shoulder.

"Nathan, you've been hit!"

" 'Tain't the first time," I said. There's times you get so caught up in what you're doing that you can get hurt some and never even suspicion it until someone tells you so. And usually it's when that person tells you about your wound that you start to feeling what has been there all along. And most times you're probably wishing you hadn't been told in the first place. Which was just how I was feeling then. Of a sudden I was remembering those two birds by the fire and how one had hit me. In all the excitement and confusion I had forgotten all about it until just now. Still, even if it was only a flesh wound, it was bringing back to me a lot of the aches in my body that I would must as soon do without. "Don't worry about me, Ellie," I said, pulling a neckerchief out and folding it in halves. "You get you a fire going and see can you get that bullet out of Lotty."

Ellie gathered some deadwood as I went through the bedroll on Ward's horse. I found what I was looking for, a bottle of what was supposed to pass as liquor, and poured some on the neckerchief before taking a long swallow for my innards.

"Where's Joe?" Lotty asked, only half-conscious.

"He's . . . he's back at the camp, Lotty. I don't think he made it." It was painful to say it, but it was the truth. Finn was one for being fair with people and trying to make them feel like they had done a lot, even when they hadn't. Me, I was in the habit of being honest with a body and the truth of the matter was that sometimes that hurt—a lot. But in a situation like this it was better she know what was probably going to happen to her husband, if it hadn't happened already.

"What happened?"

"I think he figured if he stayed behind, the Comancheros would let us go, as long as they had a hostage. Helluva trade-off." I said it slow, knowing that Ward had sacrificed his own life for my family's. It could weigh heavy on a man's mind, a thing like that. Then I got to thinking, remembering that I had only seen Ward knocked down, not shot. Maybe, just maybe, he was still alive.

I was reloading the Colt when Ellie got the fire going.

"What are you doing?" she asked, having a good knowledge of what was likely on my mind. "You're not leaving again, are you?"

"Just a social call, Ellie." When she frowned, I smiled and said, "You're always saying a body ought to be neighborly."

"You can't now," she said, throwing her arms around me again.

"Got to, woman. Pa always said pay your debts and I owe one."

I handed her the Hawken and mounted my horse.

"You take care of her and I'll be back." It didn't seem to make her feel any the more confident, so I leaned over the saddle, as though to confide a secret to her. "Look, honey, they didn't expect the three of us before, so they damn sure ain't gonna figure on one man alone coming back for the same thing. Besides, you know good and well Lije would have done the same thing."

Then I kissed her and rode off.

Chapter Thirteen

There are some things a man does because he wants to. Things like finding a wild daisy and sticking it in his hat just so's he can give it to his wife and then, after he tells her he figured it to be the prettiest thing he ever did see, maybe saying that it reminded him of her when he saw it. I did that with Ellie once and neither of us was liable to forget it for the simple thought it conveyed. Or setting your young'un on a horse and leading him around the yard awatching the joy in his face at being able to set atop a horse like his pa, and all the while thinking how you'll brag when he's grown up about how he was able to ride before he could walk. I had done that with James, too, and would be a long time in forgetting it. Those are the kinds of things a man does because he wants to, and being able to do that with my wife and son was all part of the reason for wanting to get them back so desperately.

Then there are the things a man does because he has to. And sometimes he'll do them not because he is some kind of hero like Finn's storybooks made out, but simply because it is what is expected of him. Whether it meant protecting your womenfolk and having a good healthy respect for them or lending a hand when your neighbor was in need of help didn't matter. You did what was expected of you, for it was the way of the land. And the people.

No man west of the Mississippi worth his salt ever had to go into a debate with any man he owed a favor to, or tallied up the exact date or number of times he repaid him. You might hear a man say "Much obliged," or "I owe you one," but that would be as far as it went. Other than that, well, I reckon you could say that it was expected you would help out when it was needed. If there was only one lesson to be learned on the frontier it was that no man, no family, ever survived by his lonesome. If you didn't work together, you would likely fail at what you were doing and wind up heading back east or wherever it was you came from. The land was that big, that hard.

So I had to go back, had to get Ward. Odds were he didn't figure me for a fool crazy enough to do it, but the man deserved at least one last chance. And more and more it was looking like I was the only one who could give it to him. Besides, one phrase that Lotty had said stuck in my mind, and when you got right down to it, that one sentence was the reason I was going back. "Keeping your family from winding up the way his did . . . that's what Joe Ward has to do," she had said. And that he had in no small measure. I recalled a quote from the Scriptures that I had heard long ago, the one about how noble it was to lay down your life for another man. I always figured it took some doing to do something like that, and looking back on what had just happened, it wasn't something you up and turn tail and run on. Nosiree. By God, you show the man you was worth every bit of it! And that was just what I was fixing to do.

The sun was about to break through when I got back down in that gully we had started from the first time. Checking the loads in my Colts, I once again got the feeling that something wasn't just right. In fact, this time I could see it wasn't! Off to the east was a small war party of Indians, no telling whose tribe they belonged to in this part of the country. There might have been a couple or three dozen of them, but like I say, my eyes were getting worse. And what they seemed to be doing was parlaying with about half the camp of Comancheros. Which was fine with me, since that cut the odds in half. The bad part was that both the Comancheros and the war party were heading right for the camp. That meant I had a short time to get in and get Ward and get us out and . . . To hell with thinking about it!

I dug my heels into the mount and pulled out both Colts. We took off, that horse and me, right straight for the camp. I had the reins in my mouth and God help me if the mount stumbled and fell, for I'd be losing a whole mouthful of teeth. The sand helped some, too, for the few that were in camp didn't hear me until I was upon them. I rode through an opening, both pistols cocked, and spit the reins from my mouth. The horse was as scared as anyone else, including me, and pulled to a halt and reared back some.

"Ward, where the hell are you?" I yelled as I snapped a shot at one man grabbing for his rifle. He was dead before he or his weapon hit the ground.

I slid off the horse as soon as he had his feet back on

the solid ground, to keep from making myself any more of a target than I already was. Two shots rang out then, one of them from where Ward now stood, a rifle in his hand, the other from my left. I felt the impact of the second shot as my thigh began to feel as if it had been hit by a small mountain. I buckled to one knee and pulled off a shot at the one who had shot me. He fell, too.

"You all right? What the hell you doing here?" Ward asked all in one breath, keeping his vigil as he spoke. The shooting inside the camp had ceased as Ward said, "I think you got 'em all."

Quickly, he went to two of the downed men, pulling neckerchiefs and several pieces of rawhide from their pockets. When he came back, the blood in my thigh was coming out at a good, steady pace.

"Fix you right up," he said and produced a bottle of whiskey from out of nowhere, turning the neck down right over the wound. The yell I let out should have convinced the Indians approaching camp that there were others inside, although it wasn't meant that way. "The only joy in my life," Ward said, smiling as I grimaced in pain. Then, just as quickly, his smile was gone and he helped tie the neckerchiefs in place.

While he was doing that I reloaded the Colts again and managed to climb onto my mount. Ward had found a spare mount someplace in camp and I pulled the reins on my horse when Ward grabbed my arm.

"You still ain't said what brought you back." He sounded determined to find out what madness had brought me back when it was all too evident that he had done what he did for the sake of my wife and son . . . and me. Me, I had some interesting questions to ask, too, but they would have to wait.

"This ain't the time or place for a discussion," I said, jerking my arm free and pointing to the large group of riders nearing the camp. "Not lest you want to die doing it, hoss."

Finn liked to quote that Shakespeare fella and all that fancy writing and speechifying he did. One quote I remembered had something to do with discretion being the better part of valor. Now, Finn is smart, you understand, but sometimes he gets about as long-winded as the writer he's talking about. And most of us out here were too damn blunt to get flowery, so not being as educated as my brother, we had our own way of looking at what this Shakespeare said. We just figured that there was times when it was better to pull your freight than it was to pull your gun. And friend, I'll tell you, this was one of those times.

Ward and me lit out of there like it was Ezekiel himself after us, and it was about then that we started getting shot at. Ward was keeping right up with me and I only looked back once after feeling a *shoosh* of air pass my cheek. They were still within rifle range, but it wouldn't be long before we were free. Shortly, the shooting stopped and it crossed my mind that neither the Comancheros nor the Indians had given chase once we left their camp. The only reason I could conjure up was that they wanted to count their own booty and see how much we took.

Ward still had a hard, calloused look on his face, but I figured that it would soften some once he saw Lotty. When we neared camp, I was the first one to dismount. Or, at least, I tried to dismount. In the excitement of the chase, I had forgotten about the wound and nearly collapsed as I slid from the saddle, grabbing hold of it for support.

"Daddy," James said, coming over to me. "The lady's asleep." I knew he thought he was being helpful, but there was a sad look on Ellie's face as she rushed to my side to help me.

I hadn't seen Ward dismount, but there was an ashen look to his face as he stared at Lotty lying on the ground. At first I thought it was seeing her like that that had caused him to lose his color. But as he limped slowly to her side and knelt down beside her, I saw a dark-red mass of blood just below the back of his belt line. It had to be a painful wound, but from the look on his face and the desperation with which he clutched her hand in his, I'd a notion he would never know as deep a pain as he was feeling now.

"She died not too long after you left, Nathan," Ellie said, putting an arm around me as she helped me to a spot not far from a fire she had built. "The bullet was simply too far in to get at."

"I know you did your best, honey."

The wound in my thigh felt as if someone had taken my bowie and laid it over a fire for a minute or so and then stuck it in me and left it there. The intense burning sensation was more than I had ever felt before. Then, when she set me down, I yelled out "Damn!" and remembered why.

"Are you all right?"

"Yeah," I said. "It's just that the bastards shot me in the same place as last time."

"Bad habits," Ellie said with that devilish smile she could put on when she wanted to. I never could stay mad at her for long when she smiled, so in a way I reckon it helped. At least it took my mind off the situation as she began to probe for the bullet.

It had been at San Jacinto in '36 when I got shot in

the thigh, in nearly the same spot, in fact. The wound healed but there were times now when I thought I could tell just when and how much it would rain, or as well as any medicine man ever could.

I didn't mention it, but I was hoping Ellie wouldn't be too long in getting that slug out, for there was little doubt in my mind that we would soon be having visitors of one type or another, and none too friendly, I was figuring. That meant we had to get out of here before we all wound up dead instead of just wounded.

"Don't cry, mister," I heard James say, standing across from Ward. "She's only sleeping." He said it innocently, the way only a child can say such things, and it crossed my mind that maybe that is why parents always remember the little kid in you.

"Sure, son. She's . . . only . . . sleeping."

Ward wasn't what you'd call crying. He just knelt there, looking like what he was then . . . a big, helpless man, with tears rolling down his face.

"She said something before she died," Ellie said, finishing up her patchwork on me. I noticed that she seemed quite serious when she said it. "She said, 'Tell him I played the hand through, right to the end.' Does that mean something? Was she—"

"She was a friend, Ellie. A good friend. Now, get me on my feet." When I was on my feet, I smiled at Ellie and kissed her on the forehead. "I'll tell you about her sometime. I think you'd have liked her."

The red blotch of blood on Ward's back had spread considerable. Most men would have been cussing a blue streak with a wound like that, but not Ward. He still held Lotty's hand, although the tears were no longer visible. Now there was simply a blank stare of disbelief on his face as he looked down at her.

"Ward, we've got to go," I said, approaching him. "Better let Ellie take a look at your back before we go."

"I loved her, Callahan. I really did." He said it with a desperateness, as though I had to know that one fact about him.

"I'm sure you did, Mr. Ward," Ellie said. Then, glancing off into the distance, Ellie frowned. "Nathan."

I turned to see what looked like four or five of the Comancheros and an Indian brave headed toward us at a gallop. Ward must have seen them at the same time I did, for we both drew our guns. Then, realizing they were out of range, I put mine back and asked Ellie for my Hawken. When she handed it to me I took aim and squeezed the trigger, then set the butt plate on the ground and began to reload as one of the Comancheros flew from the saddle.

"I'll do that," Ellie said, taking my rifle, powder horn and ball pouch.

"Just like old times," I said to her, remembering San Jacinto and how she had proven her worth by standing there as calm as ever while a hundred of Santa Anna's Mexicans came charging at our wagon. There was lead flying all over the place, but Ellie stood her ground and went on reloading while Lije Harper and me and old Cooper Hansen kept afiring. The odds were considerable better this time, but it was still the same situation. We had no cover to hide behind and that meant only one thing. It was fight or fall.

The pain in my leg was becoming unbearable, but I reckon the thought of dying is worse and you tend to forget 'most everything else when your life is at stake. As Ellie took the Hawken, I pulled the Colt and, steadying it with both hands, fired at another of the Comancheros. I had aimed at his head, figuring to fire just a mite high, but it wasn't high enough. The bullet must have struck his horse, for the man and horse fell to the side as one, it looking like the man was trapped under the mount. Ward had pulled out his own Paterson and hobbled over to my side before doing his own shooting, knocking a third Comanchero from the saddle.

Two things happened then that I didn't expect. The first was that the remaining two Comancheros and the brave pulled their mounts to a halt and just stopped for a moment, staring at us. It was a totally unexpected move, one that shook me as much as it must have them. The second thing I didn't expect was the look on Ward's face. It was the same satisfied grin I had seen on him back at Plum Creek when we fought the Comanches. The man was a fighter to be sure, and perhaps had never been as at ease or more comfortable as when he was doing in some common enemy. I had seen men like him before, men who killed for the sake of death, but I knew that Ward had a different look about the whole thing than those others did. His was a personal vengeance and nothing was going to stop him.

Abruptly, the riders turned and headed back to their camp. Ward looked at me, the smile turning into a frown, as though to ask what had happened.

"Beats the hell outta me," I said. "But no matter. At least it bought us time to get out of here. Ellie, give me a hand getting in the saddle. Come on, Ward, let's go."

Ward reloaded his pistols while Ellie gave me a boost up into the saddle, then looked at me in that maddening way of his, a pistol in each hand.

"Can't."

"What do you mean, can't?" I said, getting mad. "Ain't nothing else to do."

"Son," Ward said, looking at James, "I'll bet you're just big enough to ride that horse over there." He pointed to the smallest of the mounts.

"Yes, sir," the boy said, filled with enthusiasm. "My pa says I can ride real good."

"Then why don't you take her," Ward said. "And hold on tight." He glanced down at his pants leg, the blood continuing to spread on his clothes. "I can't leave now, Callahan. Can't leave her. Not to them heathens." To Ellie he said, "Ma'am, I'd appreciate it if you'd mount your horse and get your husband out of here and to a doctor someplace. He's too good a man to leave to fight impossible odds. And you're too pretty a lady to be without him."

He shook his head, the way a man does in the morning when he's wanting to see the world clear-like but his eyes ain't focused yet. Then he turned to his side, held up one of the pistols and shot his horse. As the animal fell, he kneeled down beside it.

"Got to have some kind of protection," he reasoned, knowing the Indians and what was left of the Comancheros would be coming from that direction.

"Callahan, I've been dying for some years now. Might say I been going through the motions a lot. Wasn't much left after my family was gone . . . except Lotty." Slowly looking down at the blood on his pants leg, he added, "Now I'll be rid of it." Then, in a boisterous voice, he said, "So you just tell 'em I went down fighting. You tell 'em that."

"Them?"

"Oh . . . I forgot. Nothing, Callahan," he said with a wave of his hand. "Nothing."

When he said no more I decided to ask, for I knew that "them" was the army that he was so much a part of. Or had been.

"Tell me something, Ward. That lieutenant back in the Ohio Valley, was he—"

Ward smiled. "He was being kind. Won't be a bad kid if he can control his mouth." He paused, then looked me square in the eye. "He would have took me back for desertion. Guess things were just too tame back there."

He sat back, leaning against the dead horse, waiting for what he must have known was certain death. And thinking back on it I had a feeling he probably preferred it that way. There was silence again as he reached inside his shirt and pulled out the spyglass.

"Here you go, son," he said, tossing it to Ellie, who handed it to James.

"Gee, mister, what is it?"

"Your pa will show you, but right now you'd better git."

Out in that land you could hear them when they were coming in force, long before you saw them. It was a flat land of sand and dirt and cactus and sparse water. And right then we could hear them.

"You're quite a man, Ward," I said, pulling the reins on my mount.

"So are you, Callahan. Do me a favor, will you?"

"Name it."

He smiled. "Have a drink for me sometime, will you?"

"I'll go you one better, mister. I'll make it a bottle."

Then we turned to go, and I dug my heels into the mount as hard as I could, which wasn't saying much for the one leg I had. We were half a mile away when the shooting started.

"Let me have that thing, James."

The boy handed me the spyglass and I opened it the way I had seen Ward do. Looking through it, I spotted them closing in on him as he emptied one revolver into the bunched-up warriors. He must have shot a few of the lead horses, for others were forced to jump over the fallen ones, some falling in the process. And there was Ward, pushing himself to a standing position and shooting like he never had to reload. The fact is he didn't. He only had a chance to hit one of them with his fist before he was toppled over and several came about him, one pulling out a knife to take his scalp. That was when I put down the scope and gave it back to James.

You were right, Pa, I said to myself. Thank God for men like that.

Then we rode.

Chapter Fourteen

I got feverish after a while. I never could figure out if it was the wound making me feel that way or if it was what I was thinking about Lotty and Ward. Or both.

I had never met anyone so unalike yet so similar as the Wards. From the start it seemed that they were both wanting so much out of life, but had never been able to find it in each other. I had no doubt that what Sam Walker had said about Ward was true or that it was the same man we were talking about. I never would have all of the pieces of the puzzle to put together, but there were enough to give a body a fair idea of what the man was like. Had things gone right for him he likely would have been a good soldier and made good rank as an officer. But somewhere along the line his luck had run out and the man had become soured on what life had to offer, choosing to fight the bottle or whoever got in his way toward the end, not a whole lot unlike what Jim Bowie went through. Still, you couldn't pass him off as just another man who died of wounds fighting Indians on the plains. There must have been hundreds in this land they called Texas who had died in such a fracas. And I had no doubt that after what had happened at the Council House Fight, there would be thousands more who would die the same way. It was men like Ward and Bowie, men who died fighting a delaying action that gave others time, that you'd not soon forget. Men like that, well, it's sort of hard to repay the kind of debt you owe them, but with Ward I was damn sure going to try. At the end he had admitted to deserting the army, but after what I had just seen he deserved a better label than deserter on his tombstone. I would have to get Finn to do the writing, but one way or another those people back in New York were going to know that Sergeant Joseph Ward had more sand than the Great American Desert. I owed him at least that much.

Lotty had turned out to be quite a lady, too. Not ladylike in what she could do to a man, how she could make him get riled up inside with a feeling for her, but the dependable kind of ladylike that most of us knew. I had given her fair warning toward the end, telling her it would likely get worse long before it got better, but she stayed right to the end, just like Ward did. I would tell Ellie about her someday, but like most of us tend to do with people we like, I'd probably leave out some of the darker colors and paint a more likable picture. What was important was that she knew how much of a part Lotty Ward had played in getting her back. I figured once she knew that, she would understand what Lotty meant about playing her hand out right to the end.

One thing was for sure. After the Plum Creek fight, what I had learned about them individually and as a pair was enough to give me a whole new respect for those padres back at the mission. For a while there I was beginning to feel like some father confessor, what with all the secrets they had been keeping from themselves as well as me. And I don't mind telling you that no matter how highly Ma had spoken of the priesthood and how many "good Irish boys," as she put it, had entered it, I was glad I wasn't one of them. I never had been much of a churchgoer, but if what I had heard from the Wards was anything close to what those padres heard in the confessional, well, they were likely one up on the town gossips and I never did set much stock in them. I always figured there was a good deal of difference between a gossip and a storyteller, especially when you considered that one spread rumors—usually unfounded and sometimes vicious—about people living here and now, while the other told stories about people who were mostly gone from the face of the earth. And there ain't much you can do to ruin a man once he's dead and gone. By then he has usually made his mark and, if he's worth his salt, will leave behind a goodly amount of interesting tales.

We rode hard for the better part of an hour. Or at least I think we rode hard. It wasn't as fast as I had done with the grulla coming back from Plum Creek, but then I hadn't had a side of me that felt like it was burning up and slowly spreading to the rest of my body as well. It was a steady pace we kept, and I reckon that if it was hard it was because I was feeling every gallop that old horse took. It was late in the morning, the sun starting to bear down the way it did at that time, that we spotted a waterhole and pulled to a halt. Ellie and James drank their fill, but thirsty as I was, I stayed on the mount.

"Let me help you down," Ellie said, coming to my side.

"No, thanks." I shook my head, grimaced. When she frowned, I added, "It's hard enough riding right now. I get off'n this hoss, I'm liable not to get back on. Just fill my canteen and hand it up."

The water wasn't particularly cool, but it was wet and that was what counted. Taking in gulps of air like I had been will dry out your throat like one of those unexpected northers that touch down one minute and are gone the next, so I sipped at it for a while before I took a mouthful. A doctor once told me that when you lost blood, you were losing water, too. Not that I knew what the man was talking about, but, figuring he ought to know his business, I drank near half a canteen of that water before I stopped. And it seemed to help the fever, too, for I was not as delirious as I thought I had been.

"How does this work, Pa?" James asked as Ellie filled our canteens again. I showed him how to work it, as Ward as shown me, all the time thinking of what the sergeant had done for us.

Looking down at the boy playing with his newfound toy, I could see me in him, or parts of me. There were things I wanted him to know as he got older, and what was running through my mind was something I would have to repeat later on, but for right now it seemed worth saying.

"Son."

"Yes, sir."

"I want you to remember something. It's important."

"Yes, sir." His fascination with the spyglass was gone now as he listened to me.

"Whenever you find a good friend, you stand by him. Do good by him."

"Does that mean they'll give you presents like this?"

he asked, an anxious smile coming to his face as he
held up the black instrument.

"No, son. Not always." Then I glanced at Ellie,
who had taken in the whole of it, and said softly,
"Sometimes they'll give you a lot more."

I thought I saw her eyes moisten a bit as she looked
away. It was all I needed to see to know that she
understood about Ward. Someday I figured I'd tell her
the story, but right then I knew that if I never said
another word about it she would never ask.

The memory of what I had seen on my back trail was
coming in handy now. There were stretches of desert
out here where you could see damn near twenty miles;
it was that flat. Looking off to the south, I remembered
what I had seen on the way to get Ellie and James,
knew about where the waterholes were. And, as I
recalled, there was a far stretch directly south where
they were nearly nonexistent. At least I knew what was
ahead of me in that direction. Only a fool would do an
about-face and head back toward the area where those
hostiles were camped out. And I had no use for heading
farther west, not knowing anything of the conditions
out there, either. Hell, the truth of the matter was I was
little prepared for much of anything!

That left one direction and just maybe some hope to
go along with it. Eastward there *might* be water; eastward there *might* be some of Sam Walker's or Jack
Hays's Rangers that would be a welcome sight to this
old bull. Then again, eastward *might* be the whole of
that Comanche nation Hays and his men were chasing.
There were a whole bunch of possibilities if we set out
to the east, but I figured that whatever they were, they
sure beat waiting where we were for an early grave. So
eastward we went.

The riding was done at an easy pace for an hour or so. Later in the afternoon Ellie and James dismounted and walked their mounts while I stayed with mine and let him have his head as the afternoon passed.

The time seemed to go slow that afternoon as the pain in my thigh worsened. I could feel the fever coming back, but dared not take any more water. The chances of finding any soon were slim, and the horses would need it as badly as we did if we were to get out of there alive. I remembered an old-timer telling the story of how one loner had been attacked at a waterhole and, mounting his horse, had taken an arrow high in the back of his shoulder. The man had lost blood and eventually passed out, but had so strengthened the grip on his saddle that when the horse brought him to the edge of town, he appeared all but dead, the arrow still stuck in his back. The man had made it, the old-timer said, because he had a will to survive and trusted in his horse. I had the same need to survive, but as the afternoon wore on I felt myself getting weaker, at times drifting off to sleep or dream. More than once I caught myself nearly falling off the horse, but after a bit I just let him have his head and gripped my fist underneath the saddle as that one fella had. It even got so I didn't notice the heat; I was that tired.

Most wild animals have an awareness about them that automatically tells them when danger is nearing. It is an instinct born and bred of survivors. Call it a necessary means of staying alive if you will, but in a wild land it is required, and not just of animals. Once a man left the safety of the city he had to learn to call on his own survival instincts when the occasion arose. For some it was a gut feeling they got; for others it might be the hair being raised on the back of their necks. But one way or another it is there if a man wants to remain in the land instead of winding up being a physical part of it by burial. Me, I never could quite pin it down, but it was there and it would never leave.

Maybe it was the horse snorting that woke me. Or Ellie, who was walking beside my mount, saying, "Are you all right, Nathan?" in a tone that sounded worried. But there was a pain I felt in my fist and when I looked down at it, the knuckles were turning white; I had balled it up that hard. I reined in the mount, turned an ear to listen, totally aware of where I was and what was going on.

"Listen."

Ellie cocked an ear, a frown of puzzlement coming to her face.

"A stampede?"

It was the same sound I had heard back at the camp when I had gone back for Ward. The same sound made by that war party when they had charged us as we left, the sound that let you know beforehand that they were coming. Only this sound was distant right now. As it got closer it would be louder, sounding more like rolling thunder than anything else. Only I had a suspicion it would not be a stampede or thunder at all.

"The only animal that would stampede that loud would be buffalo, honey, and I don't recall seeing nary a one coming out here."

I could see the beginnings of terror in her eyes as she imagined what else it could possibly be.

"You don't think it's—"

I nodded. "The war party that hit Ward. And if I was a gambling man, I'd bet money they've got some reinforcements. That's probably why we got as far as we have. Mount up."

I didn't have to tell either of them more than that, for they had both heard the stories about the Comanches and how they took care of hostages, especially women. And I had a feeling that with what Ellie had heard about the hostages earlier, her fear was that much greater.

I knew it wouldn't be long before those horses were gone beaver. They had already started to slow up some, and looking back once I could see dust on the horizon, outlined by the sun as it prepared to set. It would be an hour or so before it was completely down. Suddenly, it struck me that the afternoon had gone quite fast after all. It was the pain I was feeling that made me think it was agonizing.

We had one chance. We had to outride those birds and stay out of distance until the sun set. Most Indians wouldn't fight at night. Something to do with their beliefs about the holy spirit and such, as I recall. If we could stay out of their sight until then, we might be able to sneak away during the night. It seemed like the only way out right now.

But looking back, I knew even that was not to be. They were in sight now and gaining on us. And if the horses didn't give out from exhaustion, they would get shot out from under us. We were in one hell of a fix, all right, and I was damned if I knew how to get out of it.

Sometimes things just come to you. You can call it a miracle or fate, or blame it on the sun and the stars, but sometimes things just come to you. And that's what happened right then.

I near rode my horse over the edge into it and broke my neck, but the animal had the good sense to pull up even if I didn't. What I had come upon, I discovered, was a gully, much deeper and a couple, three times as wide as that one the Wards and me hid out in before we got Ellie and James free. And this one wasn't all sand like the other one. It had some jagged rock at the bottom with openings that looked large enough to consume 'most any flash flood that might take place. Likely it was an outlet to one of the many underground rivers that seemed to gobble up every bit of water they came upon and fed nearly all of the wildlife in the desert year-round. The broader bank was on the northwest side, which would give me a clear shot at whoever it was that had taken a notion to ride after me. But the backside of the wash didn't rise nearly as high as the front side, leveling off onto flat ground again after rising only a few yards. That was fine with me, for all I had in mind was sharpshooting those Indians as they came at me. I'd not get all of them, but by the time we were through, they would know they had tangled with one damned angry man.

"Give me a hand down, Ellie," I said, easing myself out of the saddle. She handed me the Hawken, which I used as a walking stick to get just below the rise in the gully. "Take those horses down to one of the sides and bring back all the ammunition and powder you can find," I told her.

"Pa, what can I do?"

It was James, and I reckon he was about as excited as the rest of us. The boy had no idea what death was, only that people like Lotty went to sleep, and I found myself wishing I could give him a gentler explanation of it. But by the time the day was out, I had little doubt he would be all too familiar with the grim reaper. As for giving him something to do, there was no reason he should not feel he was helping out, so I pointed to my rear.

"Tell you what, son. You take your spyglass and

stretch it out the way I showed you and keep an eye on that land over there. You never can tell when these fellas might circle around to our rear and attack us." It seemed like an impossibility that they would attack from any place but my front, as outnumbered as I was. But the boy wanted to help and I would at least have him thinking he was doing so and safely out of my way at the same time. I watched him as he pulled out his new toy and wondered what this land would be like when he got to be my age, if he got to be my age.

"Here you are," Ellie said, handing over the mochila. She had been surprisingly calm so far, but at that moment I thought I might lose her as she threw her arms around me and buried her face in my chest. "Oh, Nathan, I love you so. Why does it have to end like this?"

I held her close, not sure what I ought to say. But if it was the end, it was no time to be less than truthful with her.

"I don't know, Ellie. I honestly don't. Maybe it's meant to be." I kissed her softly. "But I'll tell you something. I done some thinking on it a while back and before it's all over, before this land is settled . . . well, there'll be a thousand little Alamos, battles like this by people like you and me that will never be known." I ran my rough hand along her chin and smiled as best I could when I looked down at her and said, "But I got a feeling they're all gonna be worth it. Especially when a man is fighting for a woman as beautiful as you are." Then I kissed her, and even with the sound getting louder and knowing they weren't too far off, I let it linger a bit just to feel the warmness in her. When I gave her a playful slap on the bottom and pinched her, she stood back, blushing, smiling, and shaking her head all at once.

"Nathan Hale, you're impossible."

"That's what you keep telling me." I cocked my head toward the direction of the sound. "Now let's see if we can make believers out of them."

Suddenly it was all business, both of us knowing we had said all that needed to be said. The only thing left to do now was fight. I checked my loads again, Ellie doing the same with the Hawken.

"When they get within range of these Colts I'm going to open up on them, Ellie. You keep that Hawken ready and when I give you one of these"—I held up the Model 5— "start to reloading as fast as you can."

She nodded as I gave her the powder horn and bullet pouch.

They were in sight now, coming right over the horizon at us. I had kicked away enough sand behind the break so I would be able to half stand and half lean against the embankment, exposing only the top half of me. I could only see a dozen or so in the foreground, but there could have been a thousand of them for all the dust they made. It was enough to make a body wonder if he'd ever get the chance to find out how many there were, but right then I only had one thought in mind, and that was how many I could kill.

They let loose with a volley of arrows about the same time they were in range and I opened up on them with my pistol. I started out shooting high, figuring to hit one of the mounts if I couldn't get its rider. It was a waste of good horseflesh, but if it had the same resulting confusion as before, it might be the only way to keep from being overrun. It had the partial effect that I wanted but didn't stop some of the more fanatical from closing in as I fired directly at and hit three riders with my last rounds from the first Colt.

I was reaching for the second in my waistband when I heard the deafening boom given off by the Hawken as Ellie shot one brave to our side who was running for James. Like I said, Ellie is quite a woman. But then, I reckon the mother in any woman would have done that.

I knew it would only be seconds before it was hand to hand as I fired off three quick shots, missing only once. But then they did the damnedest thing, pulling to a complete halt when they were only thirty yards from us. It was as if they were dumbstruck, as though one of their gods foretold of ill will if they went any farther. Still, it wasn't the time to be outthinking these renegades; there'd be plenty of time to think . . . if I stayed alive! So I fired off the last three shots as quick as you please while they sat there for what couldn't have been more than a few seconds but seemed an eternity. All three shots were good as I turned to Ellie for the Hawken. But I never did get it. An arrow took the hat off my head at the same time I saw Ellie bring that old bull rifle to aim and take another Indian from his saddle.

Then they turned tail and ran!

I squinted, watching them go, then turned to Ellie, who seemed about as confused as I was as to why they had left.

"I don't understand," she said, reloading the Hawken.

"Me neither, but I ain't gonna question it."

"Pa, look!" It was James to my rear. He had the spyglass to his eye, looking at what I could see in the distance as only another dust cloud produced by more riders. The first thing that ran through my mind was just what I had told James earlier. They had circled around behind us!

"Not again," I said, quickly grabbing the powder horn from Ellie as I began to reload. I had two of the cylinders reloaded when James yelled out again with some amount of joy in his voice.

"It's Uncle Sam, Pa!" It stopped me cold and I found myself squinting at the horizon, trying to get a better look. And by God, he was right! About half of the Rangers who had been out to our place had been labeled "uncle" by James. Most of them were a gruff, hard-riding lot, but every one of them had an appreciation for a family on the frontier and the importance of keeping it safe, so treating my son like someone special had become second nature to them. Besides, it was always good for another invite to one of Ellie's meals.

When they got a bit closer, I could see there were only six of them now that all of the dust had gone. They must have tied sagebrush to the backs of their mounts and come riding hell-for-leather when they heard the shooting, figuring it was a white man in trouble, for few Indians yet had more than their bows and arrows.

"Well, I'll be damned," I said, finishing the reloading.

James was right.

It was Sam Walker with a handful of his men.

Chapter Fifteen

"Somehow, I knew it was you," Sam said as he dismounted and gave Ellie a hug. Then, looking down at her, he added, "You know, he's got the loudest guns in the territory and can't keep out of trouble, to boot."

"Bad habits, I keep telling him." She smiled.

"Horse apples, Sam," I said, feeling the strength leave me and taking a seat. "I was test-firing these." I held up the Colts.

"And since those Indians were chasing you, you decided to use them for targets."

I shrugged. "Seemed about the best thing to do at the time."

Sam smiled, shook his head, and gave some orders. It was near sunset, so he had a couple of the men collect some deadwood, while another rounded up some medical supplies and gave Ellie a hand at checking my wounds. The bleeding had started some again, but after a fire was going, Old Bob, the whiskered old coot who was attending my wounds, pulled out his bowie and did a quick job of cauterizing it, producing a small bottle of whiskey as he did.

"Here," he said, handing me the bottle after he had taken a long pull, "have a snort. It'll steady your nerves."

"What brought you out this way?" I asked Walker as Ellie and Bob bandaged my wound. "How'd you know where to find me?"

"You don't think we come out here to save you, do you?!" Old Bob said in disgust. "Nosiree! Ain't nobody wanting to save someone as ugly as you!" He talked as crusty as he looked, in a way reminding me of Cooper Hansen. He was one of those old coots who would complain about everything until he died but who could be counted on when the chips were down to give his all. "Why, if them Comanch' was to take your scalp and hang it in a wikiup, Nathan, it'd put such a curse on the Injuns out here that they'd *never* fight again . . . and that'd take all the fun out'n my life." All of a sudden he got real shy, a blush coming to his cheeks as he turned to Ellie, taking off his hat. "We come to get you, Miss Ellie." He said it as if he were a young man courting a woman for the first time.

"Me!" Now Ellie was blushing, for it wasn't often she got flattered like that.

"Yes, ma'am. Couldn't stand to lose a woman cooks as good as you do! Speaking of which," he said, clearing his throat.

"Why is it that whenever you men aren't fighting, all you can think of is eating?"

"Why, it purely takes the energy out of a man, darling," Bob said, then, guiding her by the elbow, he added, "Now lemme show you what I've got in the possibles bag."

"He's about right, you know," Sam said after the two had left.

"How's that?"

"After we were out a couple of days, I mentioned that you had gone after Ellie and James and, since we had found nothing in our scouting, the boys figured you might need a hand."

"Well, you came along about the right time, hoss. I was near ready to say my prayers when you showed up."

"Do you think they'll be back?"

"I'd count on it if I were you, Sam. When they turned tail to leave, I spotted a couple of Comancheros who had positioned themselves as outriders to the whole fight. I raided their camp and I've got a hunch that as long as they can keep those Comanches fired up, they'll stick around until they see me dead."

"We'll be ready for them, then, when they decide to try making good on that offer. Don't forget, Nate, we issued out those new Colts you brought back, the rifles as well as the Model Fives." I'd almost forgotten about those extra guns, but now, taking a gander at their mounts, I could see that each Ranger had one of the new Colt repeater rifles, and most were carrying at least one of the Model 5s. "By the way, Nate," Sam said with a grin, "now that you've 'test-fired' the new Colt, what do you think of it?"

"It's a fine piece, Sam, just like Colt said it would be. It holds together better than the original Paterson and the bigger slug and heavier load give a man more firepower. That loading rammer makes it a lot faster to get this pistol in action, too.

"You know, Sam, maybe you ought to go into partnership with Colt. With his knowledge of guns and your knowledge of the frontier and how we can use these things, you could probably make a fortune. Besides, Colt said he was gonna call this the Walker-Paterson, naming it after you.''

"You're joshing me." Sam Walker seemed genuinely surprised.

"Not at all. That's what the man said, for sure."

We had boiled beef, biscuits, and coffee that night, a welcome change for a man who's been living off of cold meals and warm water for as many days as I had. The food renewed my strength, so I didn't feel as feverish as I had. Thinking back, the meal wasn't all that different from the one we had had at San Jacinto the night before the battle. The volunteers had been eating boiled beef and hardtack from the time I had joined up, but it was the coffee that made the meal. We had captured it on a raft of supplies that were originally meant for Santa Anna and I reckon taking spoils that were headed his way made it all that much better. But it always seemed that it was coffee a man was looking forward to. Living in town or one of the villages, you could get a glass of wine or tequila or even some of the hard liquor that traders brought in from the States. But in a working outfit—and anything outside of town life was considered a working outfit, whether you were a farmer or rancher—it was a good, hot cup of coffee that a man put stock in. It was best at sunup and sundown for taking the chill off the start and end of a day, when a man could appreciate it most, for it was a rare commodity on this frontier.

"What are you thinking of?" Ellie asked, taking a seat beside me.

"Thinking on how much a man has to appreciate, I

reckon." I put an arm around her and gave her a hug. "Like you."

"Well, now, you weren't really all that sick after all, were you, Ranger?" she said in a deep, throaty voice and kissed me. My hand found its way to her side and she began to giggle. "Not now, Nathan. Let me take care of Jimmy first."

I watched her walk over to where Old Bob was showing James some of the things he could see with his spyglass when Sam came over with a fresh cup of coffee.

"Would you look at that," he said, handing me the cup.

"Yeah. He thinks this is all fun we're having."

"Well, Nate, that's what makes us all like him and all the other young'uns we come on."

"How's that? Family, you mean?"

"Not really." He shrugged. "You remember how it was when you first came out here. I reckon what I mean is, you lose your innocence real quick once you cross the Trinity."

The man was right. This was a land where only the strong survived, and it toughened you up quick or you died from it. So seeing kids like James having a good old time, even when things were looking bad, did sort of make a body feel better for a while.

"What ever happened to the Wards? The last time I saw them, they were heading this direction. They get lost, or did they catch up with you?"

"Oh, they found me, all right," I said with a sigh, then went on to tell the whole tragic story of what had happened. As I told the story, Sam seemed to accept it as the truth, mentioning more than once that it sounded like the way Ward would do things. When I finished, I spoke of the letter I was going to have Finn write for me.

"Tell you what, Nate, you get Finn to write it up and I'll endorse it and send it on back east," Sam said. "I still know some officers back there who can get it entered on his records. I don't think you ought to overlook any man who shows that kind of bravery." And I knew he would do just that, for Sam Walker, although he had not been born in the west, soon adopted the feeling many of us shared out here: Say what you mean, and mean what you say. You might say that it, too, was a part of the land and the people.

We finished our coffee in silence then, before Sam asked, "You figure about dawn tomorrow?"

"Likely. They'll be looking to get a jump on us. You got anything in mind?"

"Nothing spectacular," he said, "but I took a look-see at the terrain here earlier. We've got a flat run right here and then it winds around both sides of us and sort of plays out into the regular scheme of the land. What I was thinking was we could set up a couple of the boys on each side and the rest in the middle here. That way we could get 'em from three sides and knock the wind out of them."

"Sounds good," I agreed. "With that surprise element and those extra rifles, we might just put a dent in them. At least it'll cut down those seven-to-one odds."

I grabbed the Hawken and pushed myself to my feet, using it once again as a walking stick.

"Now, Nate, you know I have full confidence in you," Sam said in mock seriousness. "Why, I could pull out tomorrow with the boys and know you'd be able to take care of the whole passel of those hostiles."

"How's that?" I asked, a suspicious grin on my own face.

"Well, you know how it is, Nate. If you've only got one battle, you only need one Ranger."

He laughed, giving me a slap on the back that near knocked me over, and left. It was a brag some Rangers were starting to make, that business about one Ranger for one battle, but both he and I knew different. For storytelling, tales like that were fine. But when you came right down to it, a man would be a damned fool to try bucking odds like we were facing against any kind of Indians when he had some extra guns available to him and the men to use them as well. I had yet to meet a man whose courage was questioned because he had accepted some help from friends or neighbors in a tight spot. To do so in a land like this was downright foolish. Sam Walker knew it and so did I, so I laughed at his poking fun at me and made my way over to the other side of camp, where Ellie was putting James to bed.

"You've really taken a liking to that, haven't you, son?" I asked as James lay there with the spyglass clutched in his hand.

"Yes, sir," he said, still enthusiastic over the new toy. "Uncle Bob was showing me how to look at the stars at night."

"I'll bet," I said, for I could imagine Old Bob's imagination running away with him and the boy. "You get to sleep, son, we've got a big day tomorrow."

"Yes, sir," the boy said and closed his eyes, his hand still clutching the spyglass.

Ellie and I were walking away from camp when Old Bob met us on the way in.

"Well, now," he said, "where do you think you're going?"

Ellie started to flush and I was feeling the back of my own neck getting hot my own self.

"Scouting the terrain, Bob," I said, growing a bit impatient with the old coot.

"Scouting the terrain?" He paused a moment, a puzzled look on his face, then it hit him. "Oh! Scouting the terrain! Right! I see! Well, uh . . . I'll have to see if the boys got a deck of cards. And if they don't, I know I do." Then he walked away, mumbling to himself, "Scouting the terrain."

Sam was right, it did wind around a bit to the side, so we kept walking until we were out of sight of the camp. The sky was clear and I could see where James would have had fun looking at the stars close up, for the moon makes them stand out when it shines bright. I was still using the Hawken to get around on, but didn't even notice it as we walked.

"Strange," I said when we stopped and I had set the rifle aside.

"What?"

"Out there in that fight, I could hardly feel a thing in my leg when we were having a go at it. Must be something in a man's body that makes him forget about everything else when he wants something bad enough . . . like staying alive."

"Why do you say that?"

"Because right now I'm with you and I ain't feeling any pain in that leg, either. Reckon they's something else in a man that takes away the pain . . . like looking at a beautiful woman."

"Oh, Nathan," she said, throwing her arms around me, "I missed you so. I was so lonely . . . and scared."

"It's been a long time," I said before I kissed her, remembering that it had been four long months I had been away from my family and that having to go after Comancheros and Comanches was one hell of a way to meet them on getting back. "I missed you, too, Ellie. A lot."

"Lotty," she said, slowly. "Did . . . she . . ."

"She wanted to," I said, tracing her chin with my hand again as I lifted her face to mine. "But I didn't."

Then I kissed her long and hard and we never said another word. There was no need to.

Chapter Sixteen

She woke up while I was trying to get on my feet, using the Hawken to do it. I had in mind to stand there all day and just look at her, but I knew there were other things to do. It was still dark, a couple of hours before daylight, I guessed, and we had some preparing to do.

"I'll make the coffee," she said as we entered the camp.

"Already done, Miss Ellie," Old Bob said, a sly look to him. So far he seemed to be the only one in camp awake. "That's quite some terrain out there to scout, ain't it? You did, er, scout the terrain, didn't you, Nathan?"

"Every inch of it, Bob, every inch." Even in the semidarkness Ellie's blush showed.

"Amazing how fast he heals, Miss Ellie, purely amazing." Then, with a slap on my good shoulder, Bob said, "A woman will do it ever' time, boy, ever' time." He raised an eyebrow, looked Ellie up and down, then left, muttering, "Yes, sir, that is some terrain, some terrain."

Within a matter of minutes Old Bob had the camp roused and Ellie was pouring coffee for all.

"What do you mean, we're burning daylight?" the youngest recruit asked, still half-asleep. "It ain't even light yet."

"That's it, boy! You gotta do as much as you can afore the light! That way you won't burn none!" Old Bob let out a gruff guffaw as the younger man hopelessly shook his head and accepted a cup of coffee.

I was holding the coffee in one hand, leaning on the Hawken with the other, when Sam Walker refilled his cup and commented on it.

"I'll be all right, Sam," I said in reply. "Been through tougher times than these." He knew good and well I was talking about San Jacinto, for I'd told him about it often enough. But truth be known, I was likely in a worse way now than back then. At San Jacinto I had gotten shot twice, but it was during the battle itself, and when it was over—all eighteen minutes of it—there was a doctor on the field to take care of me. Now I was in the second day of carrying some lead around with me in one form or another and although I wouldn't admit it to anyone, not even Ellie, it hurt like hell. My body was stiff and my leg and shoulder hurt when I moved them, but something told me that men who had been hurt worse had fought harder in other times and places, so I had no reason to complain. In a short while I would find out how long I could stand the pain, for, as the day before, it would all come down to one final fate.

Fight or fall.

When I asked Old Bob if he still had his medicinal liquor, he said, "Sure," and offered me the bottle. He must have figured I would only take a nip, for after I had taken a couple of healthy gulps, he pulled the bottle from my lips and finished the rest himself.

"You ain't the only one who's gonna need steady nerves," he said indignantly before walking away. He was quite a character, Old Bob. Even in times like these the man was able to show a lighter side, and I had to admit it gave me as much relief as the whiskey did.

Walker set up his men as he said he would, three to each side of the embankment. He joined one group and left Old Bob to me and Ellie at the same spot I had held the day before, facing the head-on charge. Bob dug out a small area to his left and instructed James to stay there until the shooting was over. When the boy asked what he could do, I gave him the Hawken and told him to hang on to it until I needed it. Then we waited as the sun made its ascent into the sky.

The only trouble with first light is your eyes are going from one extreme to another and they sometimes play tricks on you, making you see things that aren't there as well as those that are. Only one aspect could make that worse and that was the fact that the Indians knew it as well as you did. And they could do a damn good job of using it when they wanted to. And it was this morning that they wanted to.

There were a half dozen of them that came in first on foot. We didn't see them until they were almost on us and one of the Rangers fired the first shot. I gut-shot the first one, who rolled over on top of me, and would have been sliced to pieces by the second one had it not been for Old Bob. For an old man he was a spry one, for no sooner had he back-shot the warrior than he gave the Indian a boot in the rear, causing him to fall beside me rather than atop me, where I would likely have felt his knife.

There was shooting everywhere now as Ellie helped me back to my position, and by the time I was there the six who had come at us either lay dead or had disappeared into the desert.

"Thanks, pard," I said as I handed Ellie the first Colt to reload while Old Bob did the same to his repeating rifle.

"Shoot, boy, I'd a done it for anyone, even someone ugly as you." His guffaw was the only sound to be heard at the moment as we waited for what we knew would come all too soon.

They came riding at us, nearly the same number I thought I had seen the day before. It was going to be root hog or die now, but as much as I wanted to fire, I waited. Sam and I had agreed that he and his men would open up from the flanks and thin their ranks some until the lead warrior came within pistol range. At that point it would be up to Old Bob and me to see what we could do while the others reloaded.

Every one of those Rangers could shoot like a Kentuckian and showed it. That was one brag about the Texas Rangers that was anything but idle. Six Colt repeaters went off and six horses were soon riderless, those who had ridden them now dead. If there were indeed forty of them, we had just cut the odds down a notch. And as far as I could tell we hadn't lost a man. Yet. Bob and me took out the first two leaders, he with his rifle and me with the Model 5. We had to duck right quick, for the horses kept acoming, jumping right over us into the gully and running free. As I looked back, two more horses jumped us, these with riders, one throwing a lance that landed on the heel of my boot. I

was about to turn to fire at them when Bob yelled out,
"Watch the front!" and turned around to fire at the
mounted warriors.

I fired twice, bringing down two more Comanches as
a third one rode past me into the gully. I was praying to
God Old Bob was fast enough to draw a bead on them
before they did the same to me, at the same time
wishing the Rangers would open fire again. I had a
sudden feeling that "thinning their ranks," as Walker
had put it, was now being left to me alone. I emptied
the Colt into the continuous flow of warriors and horses.
It seemed that all about me now there were horses and
riders with none too friendly looks on their faces.

I handed the empty Colt to Ellie in exchange for a
full one, proud that the woman beside me could per-
form as steady under fire as she did. I was about to turn
back to the front when those Colt repeaters started
firing again. Out of the corner of my eye I thought I
saw Old Bob and when I turned completely around it
confirmed that what I had seen wasn't false at all. The
old man lay against the embankment, a lance in his
stomach, a look of death on his face. Yet he was still
firing his repeater, taking a bead on whatever of the
half dozen Comanches now in the gully he could find. I
forgot about the frontal attack now, trusting it to the
others on the flanks. As steady as I could I took aim on
the nearest brave and fired. He toppled from the back of
his horse, dead before he hit the ground. A second and
third fell in as many shots, but I soon found the smarter
ones had dismounted and were now milling with the
horses, waiting to find a victim. I saw a pair of legs
behind one of the mounts and fired, hitting the man in
the ankle. When he fell I shot him dead with a bullet
through the heart. Another horse jumped the embankment,

the horse's hoof barely missing my shoulder as it did. By the time the horse had landed I had a bead on the warrior and back-shot him as he, too, fell lifeless to the ground.

I would have exchanged the empty Colt for a fresh one but things were happening too fast and Ellie was still loading the one I had given her. What appeared to be the last of the dismounted Comanches was making his way to Old Bob now. He had a hunting knife in his hand, ready to kill the Ranger and scalp him right then and there. I only had one weapon in reach and I used it. The brave was about to ram his knife into Bob's side when my own bowie found him and eight inches of cold, hard steel cut deep in his innards. He fell to his side and I suddenly found myself on my feet, determined to get my knife, to reclaim it from him. But I only took one step when I heard her.

"Nathan!"

I turned to my right and there he was, one of those half dozen who had started this fandango, the ones who had come afoot. At first I thought he was after me, but he was a ways off for that, a second glance telling me it was James he was headed for. The boy sat there, no longer a fun-loving look on his face. Now it was one of terror. I had to get to him! I had no weapon left, but damnit, he was my son and I had to get to him. I half stumbled, half ran toward him, ready to throw myself at the Indian to save James if need be, but I never made it.

I didn't have to.

What seemed like a lone shot in a vacuum of silence rang out behind me as the warrior fell dead, the knife in his hand landing close to James as he did. When I turned, I saw Sam Walker holding a smoking Colt Model 5 in his fist.

"Shoots high and right," he said as calmly as if nothing had happened. "I was aiming for his belly button."

From where I stood I could see where the ball had entered, killing the man as it punctured his heart.

"Don't matter long as it does the job, I reckon." I tried to sound calm, but inside I wasn't sure what I would do next.

The shooting had stopped; apparently the Comanches had given up for now. Or else fled. There were bodies strewn everywhere, all of them hostiles except for Old Bob. As James ran by to his mother, I grabbed the Hawken from his grip and in that instant something told me it was not over yet. Not yet. I glanced around again and then I knew.

They were the same place I had seen them yesterday, holding the same positions as outriders, only this time there were three instead of two. If they saw me they made no never mind about it and that was fine with me. I took aim with the Hawken and slowly pulled the trigger. When the smoke cleared, the man I had shot at was falling from his horse while the other two turned tail to run.

"Sam, get me my horse," I said and I purely hoped he wouldn't cross me, for I was getting mad. The Indian fight might have been over, but I had a fire building in me right then that could only be put out by doing in those two Comancheros. For that was what was wrong. Not the Indian attack itself, but those two birds. They were the ones I had seen kill Ward! And by God they were going to pay for it!

Ellie handed me one Colt and began to reload the other as I did the same to the Hawken. All the while James was kneeling at Old Bob's side.

"You're hurt, Uncle Bob!"

"No," he said, slowly, "just . . . tired." His hand found James's arm and he grasped it tight. "You'll do like I told you, son? Look at them stars?"

James produced his spyglass. "Yes, sir," he said sadly.

"You look hard enough, son, you'll find one with your name on it."

"Yes, sir." A tear rolled down James's cheek.

"Ellie," the old man said, his voice fading. Ellie handed me the Colt and knelt down beside the old man as he whispered in her ear. When he was through I looked down at him.

"Bob." His glance turned my way. "I'll miss you, you old coot."

"How could you miss me?" He smiled, as though at peace with the world. "Ugliest man ever born." Then his head fell to his side.

"He's not ever gonna wake up, is he?" James said, the sadness still in his voice. "Not ever."

"No, son," I said, "not ever."

Sam Walker gave me the reins to my horse then, a curious look to his face.

"You mind telling me what you're doing?" he asked as he helped me into the saddle.

"Personal business," I said, a sharp tone to my voice.

"Personal?"

"Those two hombres riding off just now are the ones that killed Ward back there. I owe him at least that much."

Part of the Ranger brag is that you be able to ride like a Comanche. Well, friend, about then I wasn't too awful sure I could ride as well as my son, much less a

Comanche. I had a fire in my leg from the moving around I had done, but the fire I was feeling inside me was burning harder, so it didn't matter. Not one damn bit! I got that horse agoing as fast as I could stand it and then I dug my heels in deeper. It was easy picking up their trail and just as easy to follow, so I rode hard for maybe half an hour. When I pulled up to rest my mount, it wasn't long before Sam Walker was reining in beside me.

"What are you doing here?" I asked.

"You said it was personal, right?"

I nodded. "So?"

The look on Sam's face was about as hard as I was feeling then. "You forgot, Nate," he said. "I fought with him, too."

"Yup," I said, forcing myself back into the saddle. "It's personal."

We rode hard for another hour then caught sight of them as they entered one of the sparse groves of cotton-wood in that area. Wasn't neither one of us, Sam or me, ever cared much for long drawn-out war councils, so we nodded to each other and began to circle the grove from opposite sides.

As much as I had been shot at of late, I was beginning to feel like bait for a trap, and as impatient as I was getting I figured one more time wouldn't make any difference. So about halfway through my circle I cut the reins a sharp right and walked that horse right into the grove. And bigger than God made green apples there they were. The two of them were on my left as I reined in my horse and leaned across the saddle, partly because my stomach was tied in knots, partly because I had a surprise in store for these two birds.

"It's your time to die, meester," the one with the

horse pistol said. He was of medium size and for my money about as ugly as they come. But the smile on his face said he held a pat hand and he was carrying his bets to the hilt and he didn't care one bit. But then, neither did I.

"Sonny, I've had people telling me that for nigh on two weeks now," I said with the impatience of a sore loser. "What makes you think you're any better than the rest of them?"

"Thees." He waved the big bore pistol in his hand. "Trow your rifle and gun to my amigo, *por favor*."

I did as he requested, knowing he had taken the bait. I had positioned my right arm across my saddle, concealing the second of my brace of Colts.

"You really liked getting those Comanches to take after us, didn't you? And kill Ward and all."

"*Sí.*" He said it as if he were letting out a long-kept secret.

"Why?" I asked, getting madder.

The man shrugged, his partner silent. "He invaded my camp. It was a personal affront. I could not let him get away with it." His grin widened then. "But as I recall, you were there, too, and caused much disturbance. So you see, señor, now it is your day to die."

He was raising his pistol just a mite higher for a head shot when a shot rang out and his partner fell backwards, as if hit by a bolt of lightning. It pulled him off guard enough so's I had the time to pull my Colt and fire point-blank into his chest. The gun bucked and sent his body slamming into one of the trees, putting him in an upright sitting position.

"What you do that for?" he asked, a glaze on his face that believed it impossible that he could be dying.

"You had my wife and son as hostages in your

camp," I said, as hateful as I had ever been. "And like you say, amigo, in my country that's a personal affront."

He was trying to raise the pistol again, trying one more time. It was my second shot that killed him.

Sam Walker came out of the trees.

"You sure took your time," I said.

"High and right, just like I said" was his only comment.

It wasn't too long after that that Ellie came riding into the grove as out of breath as her horse.

"Are you all right, Nathan?" she said, gulping air. "I heard shots."

I motioned toward the ground and the two dead men.

"They didn't fare too well."

"You didn't . . . I mean, you're not—"

"Nope," I said with a grin. "Didn't get shot. Not this time."

Renegades like those Comancheros deserved the buzzards, so we took their horses and left them where they lay. I must have had a disturbed look on my face as we started back, letting our horses have their heads.

"What's the matter, Nathan?" Ellie asked.

"Don't seem right," I said, "going through all that and losing Ward and his wife and Old Bob. 'Tain't nothing like them happy endings Finn's always talking about in his books. Nothing a-tall."

"Don't sell yourself short, Nathan," Sam said. "After all, you got your wife and son back and that's what you set out to do, wasn't it?" When I didn't answer him, he said, "Well, if you two will excuse me, I've got some Rangers to take care of. Don't take too long getting back to camp." Then he was gone.

We rode in silence for a while and I got to thinking about what Sam had said. And the more I thought, the more I knew he was right. Looking at Ellie, I knew that I could never have or ever want another woman but her and if I didn't have her, well, life would be rough. Between her and James, I had had more happiness in my life than I had ever had before . . . or ever would. That must have been what brought the smile to my face.

"What are you thinking, honey?" She had that shy, girlish look about her, the one she had whenever she knew what I was thinking but wanted to hear it from me.

"I was just remembering what I told Finn last time I saw him."

"What's that?"

"I told him if he didn't have the place cleaned up by the time you got back, you'd likely raise hail Columbia."

Her smile was warm and loving now.

"In that case, Nathan, I think we should go home."

And we did.

About the Author

Jim Miller began his writing career at age ten when his uncle presented him with his first Zane Grey novel. A direct descendant of Leif Erickson and Eric the Red, and a thirteen-year army veteran, Mr. Miller boasts that stories of adventure flow naturally in his blood.

When not busy writing about the future exploits of the Callahan brothers, Mr. Miller spends his time ensconced in his 2,000-volume library filled mostly with history and research texts on the Old West.

The author lives in Aurora, Colorado with his wife and their two children.